CW01498359

The Time Keeper

A DI Erica Swift Thriller, Volume 11

M K Farrar

Published by Warwick House Press, 2023.

THE TIME KEEPER

First edition. May 21, 2023.

Written by M K Farrar.

For Jasmin

I promise there are no limbless bodies in this one!

Chapter One

He opened his eyes to pitch-black and the hollow trickle of water somewhere nearby. A dank scent lingered on the air, like something organic rotting. A chill touched his skin, eliciting a rush of goose bumps, and he shivered.

Where was he? What had happened?

He tried to move but was only rewarded with the clinking of metal and the sense of being weighed down.

What the fuck?

He was sitting, that much he could tell, in some kind of hard chair, his spine bolt upright against the backrest, his bare feet on a cold floor.

A steady beat thudded inside his head, as though he could feel his heartbeat in his brain, and it thumped against the inside of his skull with every beat. His muscles juddered with a combination of fear and the cold.

He attempted to stand, but though he could lift his backside off the chair, his arms and legs refused to budge. The clinking sounded again, sparking a memory. Chains, he was sure of it. Was he really chained to this chair? Who had put him here?

He tried to think back to what he could remember. His alarm had gone off at six a.m., as it did every weekday morning, so he could get up and make sure the kids were ready for school on time.

His wife was the breadwinner in the home, but he didn't mind. He liked not having the pressure of worrying about keeping a boss happy—the only boss he had was his wife, but he was content to take a back seat and let her do things. He liked being able to attend the kids' sports days and concert performances. How many dads living in London got to do things like that?

But had he done the school run that morning? He desperately tried to think back, but all the days seemed to blur into one. Had he left his three-storey home in Islington? Was he still in his house? He didn't think so. Though he was effectively blind, nothing about his surroundings seemed familiar.

A fresh jolt of fear went through him. What if something bad had happened to Henry and Matilda? What if the children were here with him—wherever 'here' was?

"Hello?" he croaked into the darkness. "Is anyone there?"

Nothing.

Only the steady trickle of water met his ears. Where was it coming from? Were his feet wet? Or just cold? What had happened to his shoes?

In the solid darkness, it was hard to tell if he was imagining things.

He forced his thoughts back to the events that had led to him waking here.

He'd definitely come back from dropping the kids off at school. He remembered opening the front door, and thinking the postman had been early today, and stooping down to pick up the mail. He'd even opened one of the letters—a credit card statement that he'd read and told himself they needed to swap for a new one with a lower interest rate.

Debt was a killer.

If he'd dropped the children off at school, at least that meant they were safe. It was a small reassurance, but it was something.

Had someone been in the house when he'd got back? Had someone broken in? He had home security, but he had to admit he'd grown a little lax about setting the alarm, especially when he knew he wasn't going to be out for long.

It seemed as though that had been a mistake. A big mistake.

A low *clunk* was swiftly followed by a blinding light, so intense it was almost painful. He squeezed his eyes shut and twisted his face away. He wished he could raise his hand to shield his eyes, but it was chained to the arm of the chair.

His eyes streamed, even as he struggled to open them. Why did the light need to be so fucking bright? It was as though he was sitting under spotlights at a football stadium, but he knew that wasn't the case. He wanted to be able to see, to take in his surroundings, and try to get some idea about what had happened to him. A part of him didn't want to know, however. What would he be facing?

He was forty-six years old and had never considered himself a coward, but he did right now. He was scared. Fucking petrified, in fact. Whatever had happened to him wasn't a good thing, that much was clear.

"Richard Morrisey."

The booming voice came from all directions, as though from surround-sound speakers.

He blinked again a couple of times and then managed to open his eyes to slits, though they streamed with tears. Was it a reaction to the sudden light, or was he crying? Squinting, he peered into the light. Who was speaking? Were they in the room with him—whatever room this was?

"Say hello to your viewers, Richard," the voice said.

Richard lifted his head enough to take in his situation. Sure enough, both his hands and feet were chained to the chair. That wasn't all. The chair itself had been bolted to the floor. The floor was solid concrete, and it was damp, too. He couldn't see the source of the sound of running water, but it came from somewhere behind him.

He wrenched his arms up, rattling the chains.

"What the fuck? What is all this?"

"That's kind of rude of you, Richard, wouldn't you say?" the voice replied. "You have people watching who would like to be acknowledged by you."

"Let me out of here," Richard yelled. "This is fucking ridiculous. Who are you? Why are you doing this?"

"You'll find out soon enough."

Now his eyes had grown used to the light, he was able to look around. Was that a camera right in front of him? It felt so out of place that he almost didn't want to believe it, but it was definitely a camera, set up on a tall tripod that was also attached to the floor. Why had it been attached? Was whoever had done this worried he'd somehow get his hands on it and use it as a weapon? He couldn't see how that could happen, considering his current circumstances.

He stared down the lens, sensing he was somehow making eye contact with whoever lay beyond it.

The voice had told him to say hello to the viewers, but was the man talking about himself, and maybe whoever he was with, or was he talking about a wider audience?

Did he recognise the voice? The adrenaline spiking through Richard's system was making it hard to get a thought straight. He was in flight or fight mode, and he could do neither.

This was fucking crazy.

He raised both feet as high as he could and stamped on the floor like a toddler having a tantrum.

"Let me go! Let me the fuck out of here!"

He stamped again and yanked his arms up and down. He seemed to lose the use of his words, and they all blurred into a scream of rage and frustration. He roared and shouted, and stamped and jangled the chains, losing all sense of self, becoming a ball of raw emotion, until he finally ran out of steam.

He slumped in the god-awful hard chair, his shoulders hitching, tears running down his cheeks. He'd made all this noise, but he hadn't been silenced. No tape had been put across his mouth nor some strange gas let into the room to knock him unconscious.

It meant one thing.

No one was close enough to hear.

Chapter Two

D I Erica Swift sat at her desk and groaned at the pile of paperwork waiting for her. Around her, the office was a busy hum of phones ringing, people talking, and keyboard keys clicking.

She picked up her coffee to take a sip, discovered it was freezing cold, and huffed out a breath of frustration.

It seemed as though no matter how much she did, the mound of paperwork continued to grow. She thought that with everything being on computers these days, it would streamline things, but it was as though the powers above just came up with new shit to file instead.

Not only that, she also had to keep up with paperwork from her daughter's school and all the clubs she attended. Her personal inbox seemed to fill up as quickly as her work one these days, and what with all the spam she was flooded with as well, it was easy to miss something important. The other week, she should have gone to the school early for an event, but she hadn't even read the email.

Poppy was heading off on her first ever residential this week. Though the girl had spent probably more than her fair share of nights away from home, because of Erica's sister and her family helping out so much with the childcare, it still felt strange knowing Poppy wouldn't be home for several days. It was an activity week, where she'd be doing rock climbing and abseiling, orienteering, and hiking. She'd have an absolute blast, Erica was sure, but that didn't stop her worrying.

Erica's partner, DS Shawn Turner, approached her desk, his mobile phone in his hand. From the press of his lips and the furrow of lines between his eyebrows, it was clear something troubled him.

"We've had a call come in about something," Shawn said, hesitation in his tone, "but I'm not one hundred percent sure how to act on it."

Erica was glad for the distraction. "That sounds intriguing."

He grimaced. "I'm not even sure if it's real or if it's some kind of prank. We had a concerned member of the public call it in when it came up on their newsfeed."

She angled her head. "On their newsfeed? It's something on social media?"

"Probably best if you watch it."

Shawn handed her the phone. A video had been paused at the start, so she hit play.

Onscreen, a man sat chained to a chair. His feet were bare, but he was dressed in jeans and a t-shirt. His head was bent, revealing a balding patch on his crown. In the corner of the screen, a timer was counting down. It had sixty-seven hours and forty-three minutes remaining.

Erica frowned and glanced up. "I don't understand. What is this? Some kind of game?"

"Scroll down," he told her. "Go to the comments. There's a link to another video that doesn't appear to be a livestream. My guess is that it was recorded earlier."

She did as he'd suggested and checked the comments. There were already a lot, as were the views showing. Most of the comments were ones that made jokes, but some sounded concerned, more along the lines of 'what the hell is this?' and 'what the fuck?'

Pinned to the top was the link to another video.

Erica clicked on it, and, at first, all she could see was a black screen, but then bright floodlights turned on and the same man she'd seen in the chair reared back as though the light had hurt him.

From out of nowhere, a voice said the name, "Richard Morrisey."

The man onscreen reacted in much the way Erica thought most of them would, asking what the fuck was going on. There was a brief exchange where the voice tried to get the man—presumably Richard—to say hello to his viewers. Then Richard freaked out, screaming and thrashing around, and the video ended.

"Is this real?" She glanced up at Shawn as though she expected him to have the answer, though he'd already told her that he didn't know if it was a prank.

"Unsure, but it certainly looks real. We did a search on the name the voice said and ran it against our records. There are thirteen Richard Morriseys living in the London area, but we don't even know where this video is originating from. They could be in Scotland for all we know."

"Or it's just a hoax. Someone's playing a strange kind of game."

"It's definitely strange," Shawn replied. "I'll give them that much."

Erica thought for a minute. "Can we get a screengrab of the man's face from the video? Even if we can't match the face through facial recognition software, it'll at least give us a description. I'm guessing he's aged somewhere between forty and fifty. It'll help us narrow down the Richard Morriseys."

"Good thinking." Shawn nodded. "I guess we're going to have to find contact details for any who match the description and phone around. If we can get hold of the person, then we'll know it's not them."

She blew out a breath. "Honestly, I'm not even sure a crime's been committed here, though it is disturbing."

"The man's been chained to a chair. I'd say that's a strong indication he's there against his will."

Erica went back and rewatched the video, first the initial one where the man's name was said, and then the live-streamed version. She'd never seen anything quite like it—outside of a horror film, of course. The man's reaction seemed completely genuine, but surely it couldn't be real.

"Maybe this is a crazy promotional stunt of some kind or it's done by amateur dramatics to build up to a play or something?" Shawn suggested.

Erica twisted her lips. "It definitely does have the feel of a promotional stunt. Who was the person who called it in?"

"A woman called April Watson. She was scrolling through the internet and came across it. She clearly thought it was real enough to contact the police about."

"Does she have any priors? Any reason to think she might be trying to stir up trouble?"

"No," Shawn said. "She's a sixty-two-year-old grandmother. Retired. I can't see any motive there. I don't believe she's connected in any way."

It wasn't often Erica found herself stumped about how to handle something, but she was with this. Should they ignore it? It wasn't as though they didn't have plenty of other cases to be getting on with.

If this was a call about someone spotting a person threatening their own life on the internet, or the life of someone else, it would be easy enough to send uniformed officers around to that person's address to assess whether they needed to take the threat seriously. But in this situation, she didn't have an address to send anyone to, and it didn't appear as though the location was a person's home.

Something about the way the man had reacted when the lights had come on hadn't felt like he was acting. Quite the opposite. If he was an actor, then someone needed to give the man an Oscar right away. How he'd screamed and thrashed around, trying to free himself, seemed as genuine as anything else she'd ever seen. It had made her skin prickle with goose bumps.

He'd seem genuinely terrified.

"Is there anything about the video that gives us an idea about where he's being held?" Erica wondered.

Shawn leaned over her to study the live feed that was still playing on the phone. "It looks like a kind of concrete bunker. There's no external light. If this is a live feed, we know it's daylight outside, and has been for several hours, but in the first video, the room was pitch-black. The floors are concrete, too, and the chair has been attached to it by metal plates. Other than that, we have no idea."

Erica wasn't used to working like this. Normally, she had a crime scene she could go to, victims she could support, witnesses she could interview, actual evidence that could be gathered. What was she supposed to do with a video on social media?

"What does the timer mean?" she asked. "It's clearly a countdown to something, but what?"

It was clear neither of them wanted to say out loud what it could be. It was like tempting fate.

Shawn arched his brow. "Let's just say it's counting down to the end of the show, at least until we know anything different."

She flipped back through the phone, to the video clip that appeared to not be live, and watched it over. "Why did the speaker say the man's name? He wants people to know the man's identity. For what reason?"

"So people do their own research, maybe? If it is a publicity stunt, maybe it will bring something up."

"But it didn't, though," she said abruptly. "And if this is a publicity stunt, what is it they're trying to publicise?"

"That might be revealed later. It's like when you get those scam posts of injured animals or old people, and everyone shares them, only for the original poster to then change the post to be one selling knockoff mobile phones or something."

She lifted her chin and locked eyes with him. "Is that really what you think?"

He let out a breath and scrubbed his hand over his head. "Honestly, Erica, I don't know what to think."

She paused for a moment. "Let's try and track down this Richard Morrisey and take it from there. We can also link in Digital Forensics. See if they can get a trace on what IP address is being used. Maybe that'll at least help us pin down where the video is being streamed from."

"Good idea."

She'd dealt with some strange cases in her time, but this was definitely up there.

She handed Shawn back his phone. "Let me know as soon as you find anything."

"You don't think we should get the rest of the team involved?" he asked.

"Not yet. They're all busy with other cases, and I don't know what DCI Gibbs is going to make of all this, especially if I pull everyone else off what they're currently working on."

Shawn grimaced. "Are you going to tell him?"

Erica got to her feet. "Yeah, I'd better. If this develops into something, he's going to want to know why he wasn't informed."

"Good luck."

"Thanks, I might need it."

Chapter Three

E rica knocked on her boss's door, waiting for his familiar call of 'come', and then entered.

DCI Charles Gibbs sat behind his desk, a photograph of him and his wife to his right, and a plant that looked as though it had been overwatered sitting on the windowsill. She could see the years in his face now. Ever since he'd suffered a stroke, he seemed to have aged more quickly. With such a demanding job, he should probably be thinking of slowing down, but, despite his wife encouraging him to do just that, he refused to transition to a life of retirement.

"Everything all right?" he asked as she walked in.

He gestured to the empty seat on the other side of his desk, and she slipped into it, wondering how to go about discussing this with him.

"Honestly...I'm not completely sure. I hoped to get your thoughts on something."

"Of course. Whatever you need."

She brought up the link on her phone and slid it across the desk to him. "We had a concerned member of the public call this in."

He frowned down at the screen. "What is this?"

She filled him in on everything they knew so far, which wasn't much.

He bit his lower lip, chewing at a piece of dried skin, and then gave back the phone. "We can't be expected to police everything happening on the internet, Erica. I bet if you sat down and dug into the dark web, you'd find a whole heap of things exactly like this."

"Yes, but this isn't happening on the dark web. Everyone and anyone can view it."

"Even so, this isn't what your team has been set up for."

"We deal with violent crimes. This looks like a violent crime to me."

He gestured at the phone. "We don't even have a victim."

"We know the man's name. I've got DS Turner seeing if we can get a match on the victim's face. If it looks as though something has happened to him, then we will have a victim."

He pursed his lips and shook his head. "We're already stretched on resources. We've got both knife and gun crime on the rise in the city. I know there are cases more pressing than this one."

"I don't know, sir. Something about this doesn't feel right to me. Maybe it is someone playing a prank, but if that guy is acting, he needs to be on stage somewhere."

"And maybe that's exactly what you'll find out. That this Richard Morrisey is an actor, or hell, maybe he's even a character in a play. You've got to admit that it would certainly create an impact."

Erica stood her ground. "Then let us rule that out. The clock is counting down to something. Maybe it's the start of the play or the release of an indie film, or something similar, but if that's the case, it shouldn't take long to figure it out. After all, what's the point in promoting something if no one knows what the hell it is you're promoting?"

He let out a sigh and tapped his fingers against the desk. "It's simply not a good use of resources."

She crossed her legs and linked her hands around her knee. "You trust my opinion, don't you? There haven't been many times I've led this team astray. Give us a couple of hours, that's all I ask."

He tilted his head. "Okay, as long as I get to say I told you so when you discover it's just a publicity stunt."

She grinned and got to her feet. "Deal. I'll even buy you tickets to go and see the show."

He pulled a face. "I'm not really into horror these days. Give me a good Western any day."

"Thanks, sir," she said, retrieving her phone. "I'll keep you updated, whatever happens."

She left the office and, as she walked back to her desk, she brought up the live feed once more. The man—possibly Richard Morrisey—was sitting up now. He was focused on his right hand, doing his best to tug it out of the chains securing his wrist to the arm of the chair. His jaw was clenched, his teeth gritted. The skin around the bottom of his hand, especially the fleshy part of his thumb, had been bunched up. It was red raw from the friction of the chains. The man braced himself and yanked again and then let out a roar of frustration and fell slack again. The hand appeared bruised and swollen. Surely someone who was acting wouldn't physically hurt themselves for the role? She'd heard of method acting, but this seemed like too much.

She trusted her instincts, and right now they were screaming at her that this man was in trouble.

She used the phone on her desk to call Karl Hartley in Digital Forensics. The two of them had worked together for some time now and had a good relationship. She was fairly confident she could get him to put a rush on this, if she asked nicely enough.

"Karl, hi, it's Erica Swift."

"Hi, Erica. What's up?"

He sounded out of breath.

"Sorry, did I catch you at a bad time?" she asked.

"No, it's fine. I only just got in. Dentist appointment."

"Right." Once again, she found herself in the awkward position of not quite knowing how to explain what was happening. "I'm investigating a livestream video where it would seem as though a man is being held captive. If I sent you the link, do you think you could do some digging for me? See if you can work out where it's originating from."

"Sure, I can certainly try."

"Thanks...also, I kind of need a rush on it."

He chuckled. "Everyone needs a rush on everything these days."

"Does that mean you'll do it?" she asked hopefully.

He huffed a mock exasperated breath down the line. "Send it over. But I'm only doing this because it's you."

"I thought you said everyone wants a rush these days?"

"Yes, but not everyone gets one."

"Thanks, Karl."

She ended the call and then sent over the link for the livestream. She couldn't help but go back to watching it, studying every detail. There was something addictive about observing this poor man's distress. How many people were watching him now? As well as the countdown clock, a clicker counter that showed the number of viewers was also onscreen. Over six thousand viewers already. That seemed like a lot, though she wasn't an expert in these things. They'd only just learned of the video's existence, though, and the number had almost doubled since then. Things on the internet spread quickly. If they didn't find this man and shut this video down, God only knows how many viewers it would have by the end of the day.

Shawn, hurrying back to her desk, drew her attention from the screen.

"I've got a match on who the man might be," he said, "and I'll start by saying that as far as I can tell, Richard Morrisey has no reason to pull any kind of publicity stunt. He's a stay-at-home dad of two children who are school age."

"Is he local?" she asked.

"Yes, from London. Islington, to be precise. He's actually the husband of a local politician, Nancy Morrisey. She's a government minister."

"I thought I recognised the name." She tapped her finger against her lips. "So they have money?"

"From the address, and that both children attend private school, it certainly seems that way."

"And he's being held captive somewhere. If they're from money, that could be the motive as to why he's been taken."

"Assuming that he *has* been taken, and this isn't some kind of weird practical joke."

She exhaled through her nose. "I think we should go and pay his wife a visit, see if she knows anything."

He arched an eyebrow. "You think she might be in on this somehow?"

"Right now, who knows, but we can't rule it out. I admit it's strange, but that doesn't mean it's not possible."

"Agreed. I assume if she'd seen the live feed, we would have heard from her already, though. And if this is a ransom situation, then surely the wife would have been one of the first people to hear about it."

"It does explain the clock," Erica said. "Maybe that's the amount of time the kidnapper has given the family to come up with the ransom before..."

She didn't need to finish the sentence.

"Possibly, but why livestream it? Why not simply send the link to the wife?"

"I really don't know. Do you know where we can find Nancy Morrisey?"

He nodded. "Yes, I already made a couple of calls. Her office is located down on Whitehall Place."

Erica snatched her keys up from her desk. "I'll drive."

They headed out to the car and got on the road.

"How's Poppy feeling about her residential?" Shawn asked from the passenger seat. "She's going this week, isn't she?"

Erica navigated the London traffic, keeping her eyes on the road as she headed towards the city. "Yeah, for three nights. Honestly, she's fine. She's excited about it. I think I'm the one who'll struggle the most. It's supposed to be teaching the kids about independence, so they're not allowed to contact us directly. The teachers will call us if there are any emergencies. I guess I should be used to Poppy being away, but she's normally only down the road, and I can phone or FaceTime her whenever I want. It'll feel strange not to be able to do that."

"You'll miss her," he said. "That's normal."

"The house is going to feel very empty. I'll be all right, though. I have some microwave meals and a couple of boxed sets on Netflix to binge watch."

He hesitated and then said, his tone light, "We could do something, if you're at a loose end. Cinema, or dinner, maybe? Whatever you wanted."

She took her attention from the road briefly to shoot him a warning look.

"Just as friends," he added hurriedly, "and colleagues."

They were always treading that fine line between what was appropriate between them. It was the elephant in the room that neither of them mentioned, but that didn't mean it wasn't there.

But the thought of spending night after night, worrying about Poppy, on her own, didn't sound appealing. "Sure, why not. Dinner and a movie sounds good. Not one about a man being kept captive in a bunker with a timer counting down on him, though."

Shawn chuckled. "I don't think there's anything like that released at the moment. And do you promise not to talk about work all evening?"

She gave a small laugh. "Now you're pushing your luck."

"Okay, only part of the evening."

"If this case ends up being something big, we might not even have any evenings."

She glanced over in time to see the disappointment flash across his features. Sometimes, she wanted to say to him to go out and meet someone. She wanted for him to be happy. But at the same time, on a purely selfish level, if he met a serious girlfriend, someone he planned to have in his life, it would kill her. He was young and went out with his friends in the evenings, and she was sure he must meet women—not that he'd ever be so thoughtless or disrespectful to share any of those details with her. It wasn't any of her business. But someday soon, someone would come along who he wanted to keep around.

London traffic was slow, as it always was at this time of day, but especially heading into the centre. A throng of black cabs and red double-decker buses jostled side by side for space. On the pavement, slow-moving tourists taking photographs irritated the locals who muttered their irritation wherever the tourist stopped suddenly to admire something they'd only seen on television before.

Erica loved this city. Even though she didn't come into the centre for much more than work, she always appreciated the atmosphere of the place. It made her feel alive.

She didn't think they'd find anywhere to park but managed to find a spot.

Erica climbed out of the car and straightened her jacket. It had been a wet spring so far, and though the country was known for its bad weather, it didn't seem to have stopped raining. She was sick of getting damp every time she left the house and had almost caved and bought an umbrella, though she hated the things.

"Let's go and see what she knows," Erica said.

The office was protected by security—the Met Police Protection Command was in charge of political security, but close protection for MPs fell under the remit of Royalty and Specialist Protection—so they both showed their IDs and explained their reason for being there.

Over the past few years, security had been stepped up several levels. A couple of incidents involving men with knives—one where someone had been brutally stabbed—meant that the area was more closely guarded than ever before.

"I'll let her department know you're here," the man running the security detail said. "You'll need to wait for someone to come down to you. You can sit over there."

He nodded to a seating area.

The building itself had an air of authority, a way it resided over the rest of the city. Everyone inside moved with purpose—very busy people, all with important jobs to do.

While she was waiting, she quickly checked her phone. The man they'd identified as Richard Morrisey was still in the same position, the clock counting down in the corner. Erica glanced around, wondering if anyone else with their heads bent over their phones was also viewing the same thing, but she didn't get the impression anyone else knew about it. She scrolled down to read the comments. There was already a surprisingly large number.

<Someone needs to toss that man a key!!!>

<Is this like one of those escape artist shows?>

<Earn one thousand pounds a day from working online. Click this link to find out how.>

She rolled her eyes at that one. Were there really people who fell for that shit? She guessed there must be or they wouldn't bother posting the spam all the time.

Shawn's hand on her knee got her attention, and she glanced up to see someone heading their way.

The man approaching them made Shawn appear small. His grey suit barely fit the breadth of his shoulders, and from the way his biceps strained against the sleeves, he was clearly someone who liked to spend time in the gym. He stood ramrod straight as he walked, his shoulders back, his expression grim.

"My name is Daniel Southern. I'm the head of Nancy Morrisey's security detail. I need to know what this is about."

Erica put out her hand for him to shake. "I'm DI Swift, and this is DS Turner.

They checked each other's IDs.

"Are you aware of a video online that shows Nancy's husband being held captive?"

"What? No. Do you really think I'd be standing here talking to you if I was?"

"It was brought to our attention by a member of the public a couple of hours ago."

His eyebrows lifted. "A couple of hours? And you're only notifying us now?"

"We didn't know who the man in the video was right away. We had to do some investigating to know his identity. In fact, we weren't even sure it was real, and currently there is still a possibility that we're dealing with some kind of hoax. Speaking with Nancy Morrisey will help us establish if this is real, one way or the other."

He put out his hand. "I'd like to see the video."

Erica glanced at Shawn, and he gave a subtle shrug. There didn't seem much point in keeping it from Mr Southern, since anyone with an internet connection would be able to view it.

She pulled up the screen and handed it over.

For the first time, the big man's steadfast demeanour wavered. The colour drained from his face, and the phone trembled slightly in his hand.

He ran his hand over his mouth. "I've met Mr Morrisey. That's definitely him. You say someone's taken him?"

"Right now, we really don't know what's happening," Shawn said. "Initially, we wondered if this was some kind of practical joke or a promotional stunt, but once we were able to ID him, we realised this was most likely far more serious."

Erica pointed at the phone. "There's a clock in the corner of the screen. I don't want to take guesses as to what it's counting down to, but I think it's clear that time is quite literally running out for us to figure out what's going on here."

Daniel Southern angled his head. "You think his life is in danger?"

"We can't rule that out," Erica said. "He doesn't look as though he's been harmed, but that doesn't mean he won't be."

"But you have no idea what the motive is behind the abduction?"

"Currently not, which is why it's so important that we speak with Mrs Morrisey. We have to consider that both Nancy and the children will also be in danger."

"That's assuming his wife didn't have anything to do with this," Shawn added.

Daniel Southern arched his brow. "You think she's capable of kidnapping her own husband and then streaming it online?"

Shawn gave a small shrug. "Until we speak with her, we have no idea what she's capable of."

Daniel tutted and shook his head. "This is ridiculous. She's a good woman. There's no way she'd do something like that."

Erica stepped in. "Maybe not, but she might have an idea who is responsible. You don't know what she might be hiding. The kidnapper may well have already been in touch with her but warned her that she wasn't allowed to tell anyone or they'd kill her husband."

"She'd have told me," Daniel insisted.

"You can't know that."

Anyone could be secretive if they needed to be. And Nancy Morrisey was a politician. Erica was quite sure Nancy was able to avoid or fudge the truth, if it was needed. Wasn't that what politicians were trained to do—avoid answering questions?

Chapter Four

A knock came at her office door, and her assistant popped her head around the corner.

"Nancy, I'm so sorry to bother you, but the police are here, and they want to speak to you. Mr Southern is with them, too."

Nancy Morrisey frowned, concern instantly blooming inside her. "Is everything all right? Did something happen?"

"Honestly, I'm not sure. They said they needed to speak with you and that it was urgent."

Her thoughts immediately went to the children. Had something happened at the school? It was always a concern these days. Knife crime was on the rise, as was gun crime. Only a few days ago, a seventeen-year-old boy had been shot dead by another youth a couple of boroughs away. They lived in a relatively safe area, but nowhere was completely safe in London.

More and more recently, she'd found herself wondering if this was really the life for them. They were blessed with a beautiful home in a good location, but they could easily sell it and move to the countryside somewhere. The equity in the house alone would be plenty to live on for years to come.

She shook her thoughts from her head and focused on what was happening in the here and now. The police didn't need to be here because of something personal. They could just as easily be here because of her job. Maybe there had been some kind of threat made on the government?

An attractive detective, who Nancy assumed was around her age, entered, a younger male detective close behind her. With them was Daniel Southern, the head of her security.

The female detective had strawberry-blonde hair tied neatly at her nape, and clear blue eyes. She wore a trouser suit that was clearly bought off a rack somewhere and wasn't tailored like the ones Nancy favoured, but she wasn't going to judge.

"Mrs Morrisey," the detective said. "I'm DI Swift, and this is DS Turner. We need to speak to you about something urgent."

"Of course, take a seat."

There was a pause while everyone got themselves settled, and then DI Swift crossed her legs and leaned forwards slightly.

"Have you spoken with your husband today?" she asked.

"My husband? Richard?"

For some reason, Nancy hadn't thought they'd mention him. She'd worried about her children and about work, but he'd never crossed her mind. She experienced a stab of guilt for it.

"Is he all right? Has something happened?"

"We're trying to track him down. When was the last time you spoke to him?"

"Well..." she racked her brain... "first thing this morning, I guess. At breakfast, shortly before I left for work."

"You haven't seen or heard from him since?"

"No. Can I ask what this is about, Detective? You're worrying me."

"I'm sorry, I'm not even completely sure how to handle this myself. I was hoping that if you'd heard from him or seen him, then we could assume this was a fake."

She linked her hands primly on her desk and used her calm voice, the one she mustered whenever she needed to get the children to do something they didn't want to. "Assumed what was a fake?"

DI Swift glanced at her colleague. "I think the easiest way to do this is by showing you." She took her phone from her pocket. "I have to warn you, this isn't easy to watch."

Nancy was getting seriously worried now. What on earth were they talking about?

The detective handed over the phone, and Nancy bent her head to watch.

For a moment, she couldn't quite understand what she was seeing. It was a black screen, though she could hear the trickle of water and what sounded like heavy breathing. Suddenly, lights came on, and she found herself staring at Richard. He was wearing the clothes he'd dressed in that morning and had his eyes screwed shut against the light, his face twisted away.

She didn't understand. "What is this? Some kind of a joke?"

"We don't believe so, Mrs Morrisey."

Daniel chipped in. "This does need to be taken seriously, ma'am."

She stared between them all. "This is crazy."

"That's just the start of the video," DI Swift said, "but it's also being streamed online. It appears to be live."

"You're saying anyone can log in and watch it?"

"I'm afraid so. There's also a countdown clock that's been added to the video."

"A countdown? A countdown to what?"

"We don't know yet, but it's probably wise to assume the worst."

"You mean kill Richard?" She looked between them, praying one of them would tell her not to be silly, and of course they didn't mean that, but neither of the detectives spoke.

"Has anyone contacted you to make any demands?" DI Swift asked instead.

"What kind of demands?"

"We were hoping you'd be able to tell us."

She threw up her hands. "I have no idea. No one has made any demands of me. I didn't even know this..." she gestured at the phone, "was happening."

"Is there anything you can think of that might help find your husband?"

"I'm going to call him. He'll probably be at home, laughing at all of this."

Again, the two detectives exchanged a glance. Nancy knew what they were thinking—that if it was a joke, it definitely wasn't funny—but Richard always had had a strange sense of humour. Admittedly, it tended to be around dad jokes more than anything else. She couldn't see him pulling off something like this. Richard didn't even play computer games, and she had to show him how to add photographs to his social media posts. How could this be some elaborate hoax?

Even so, hanging on to that possibility was far more appealing than even considering for one second that this all might be real.

She got on the phone and turned her back on the detectives, not wanting to see their concerned and sympathetic expressions. The phone rang, and she pictured it ringing in the kitchen at home. Surely Richard would pick up any minute. Maybe he'd gone out for a jog or popped to the supermarket for some bits. They were forever running out of bread or milk. She'd much rather think that than he was chained up in a dark room somewhere with a faceless person threatening to end his life in less than seventy hours.

He didn't answer, so she tried his mobile number instead. This one didn't even ring and instead went straight through to his answerphone. She almost hung up but then decided against it. She listened to his voice telling her to leave a message and he'd get back to her. She hoped he would.

"Hey, it's me. I'm just phoning to check that you're all right. I've got a couple of detectives here, and...well...there's something strange on the internet. Please call me. I'm really worried."

She swiped the phone to end the call and turned back to the detectives. "He'll phone me back. I'm sure of it."

Her gaze was drawn to the other phone where the livestream of her husband continued to play. He was shouting now, screaming in fact, stamping his bare feet and yanking at the chains on his arms.

"I understand that this is disturbing for you, Mrs Morrisey," DI Swift continued, "but if you can focus for a moment and answer some questions for us, it'll help your husband."

Nancy blinked at them, feeling as though her fairly normal, boring morning had been flipped into a horror film. Surely this couldn't be happening? None of it felt real.

"No one else has been in touch with you?" the detective pressed. "No one asking for a ransom? Or anything else?"

She stared between them in horror. "This is the first I've heard of any of this!"

"Does your husband have any worries, any issues with drink or drugs, or gambling? Anything like that?"

"No. Something like that would make us vulnerable to outside influence. It's not allowed."

Erica offered her a sympathetic smile. "Just because something's not allowed doesn't mean it doesn't happen. If that was the case, we'd be out of a job."

"I understand what you're saying, but Richard really isn't like that. He's a good, steadfast kind of man. I don't think he's ever had so much as a speeding ticket."

"We do have to consider the possibility that we're dealing with a fake video. I'm sure you've heard of deep fake technology? It does exist, and it's frighteningly good. There's a chance none of this is real."

She found her voice. "He's wearing the same clothes as he had on this morning. If this was fake, how would whoever had faked it know what he'd been wearing?"

A wave of heat and nausea swept through her. Her heart was beating too hard, and her palms and brow prickled with sweat. The floor of her office suddenly didn't seem solid beneath her. She felt like she'd got off a fairground ride—not that she'd been on one of those for years—and couldn't find her balance.

She planted her hands on the side of her desk, trying to stay upright.

Her head was swimming. What was she going to say to the children about where their father was? What if the press got hold of this and decided to camp outside her front door? It wasn't as though you could keep anything secret these days. The kids both had mobile phones and were bound to be sent links to whatever the fuck this was.

"Oh my God, this can't be happening. It can't be happening."

She was barely aware of the detectives' voices around her, they sounded so distant, like she was underwater, or maybe they were. But their firm hands helped her into her chair, and she found herself folded over, her head between her knees as she gasped for oxygen.

She wasn't the type of woman who had panic attacks. She was sensible, a doer, someone who had their head on straight. People always said so.

In the distance, someone told her secretary to fetch her some water.

"Take some slow breaths. You'll be all right."

She didn't feel like she was going to be all right. And what about Richard? He must be terrified.

She loved her husband. They'd been together so long, she couldn't picture her life without him in it. Of course, he did things that made her want to smother him with a pillow at times, but she was fairly certain she could be equally annoying. He'd been so supportive of her. Maybe it was a cliché, but he'd been her rock over the years. When the children had been small and she'd hated being at home, he'd been more than happy to step into the position of being the main carer. Even when she'd felt like it made her a terrible mother, he'd assured her that she was a great role model for them both. She hoped that was true.

She suddenly thought of something that yanked her out of her panic attack.

"The children!" she cried, sitting up. "He was supposed to take them to school this morning. What if they didn't make it? They might be in danger as well."

"Have you heard from their school to say they haven't come in? Wouldn't they contact you if something had happened that was out of the ordinary?" Erica remained calm, clearly doing her best to be the voice of reason in the face of Nancy's rising panic.

"Yes, yes, of course they would have." She pressed her knuckles to her lips. "The school would have phoned me right away if they hadn't shown up. He must have dropped them off then. I think it's still best if I check though."

"Of course."

They all waited while she got back on the phone and placed the call to the school. It only took her a matter of a minute to confirm that Richard had dropped them off as normal.

Nancy filled the detectives in on the information.

"Thank you," DI Swift said. "What's your husband's normal routine after taking them into school?"

"I-I think he goes straight home. Has some breakfast, does a bit of housework. He runs everything to do with the house. I don't have time to do it."

"I understand," Erica reassured her. "I had a similar setup with my husband. Do you think he might have gone straight home after he dropped the children off?"

"I think so, yes."

"Does he drive or walk?"

"Drives. The school is a couple of miles away."

"So, if he made it home, his car would be in the drive?"

"Yes, unless he went out again."

"Do we have your permission to search your house?" the detective asked. "We need to narrow down the location where your husband was taken from. It might help us find him and figure out who is responsible."

She wiped tears from her eyes. "Yes, of course. I've got nothing to hide."

"It would be helpful if you have the keys."

"Yes, take them. Do whatever you need to."

"Here's my card," DI Swift said, placing it down on the desk. "If you hear anything from whoever might have your husband, please call us right away."

Daniel Southern stepped in. "Mrs Morrisey and her children will be taken to a safe location. Until we know what we're dealing with, we're going to have to treat this as a threat to the whole family, and possibly even the government as well."

DI Swift eyed him. "You think this might be political?"

"I'm sure you've seen the number of protesters we get here on the news. They're forever doing crazy stuff, gluing themselves to pavements or climbing the damned building. It was the first thing my mind went to."

"But what could they achieve by abducting the husband of a politician?"

He pursed his lips. "Maybe it was easier than abducting the politician herself?"

Nancy sensed all eyes turning on her, and she fought to hold back the panic threatening to take over again.

Chapter Five

E rica and Shawn left the office.

"Either she's also an excellent actor," Shawn commented as they walked back to the car, "or she had no idea what had happened to her husband."

"Maybe the husband has been hiding something from her?"

In Erica's experience, it wasn't uncommon for someone to hide a secret life from their spouse. But currently, she wasn't sure who was more likely to be hiding something, Nancy or Richard, or if they were both completely innocent.

"Possibly, but I don't think she's involved. It seems strange that she's not been contacted at all. The kidnapper must have a motive. Could it really be political in nature?"

They wove around a group of tourists all taking selfies in front of the street sign.

"It's feasible," Erica said. "Someone's put some thought into this. Did you notice that the chair Richard is sitting on is bolted to the floor? Plus, there's the lighting and camera equipment in the room with him. This wasn't a spur-of-the-moment thing."

"Could Richard have been a spur-of-the-moment victim, though? Did the kidnapper set all this up with him in mind, or did he just catch their eye? Middle-aged, white, married men don't normally become the victims in this sort of thing—"

"This sort of thing?" She raised her eyebrows. "Have we ever seen this sort of thing before?"

"No, but you know what I mean. People normally prey on those who are weaker than themselves. Unless there's a specific reason for them to have been taken."

They reached the car, and Erica got behind the wheel.

"I do agree," she said. "We need to get over to the home address, see what we can find."

He glanced over at her. "I hope they're able to protect the children from what's happening to their father. I can't imagine how they'll feel if someone shows them the video."

"Hopefully, Daniel Southern and Mrs Morrisey will get to them before that happens."

"I don't know. I'll bet every other kid in that school has a smart phone now."

She agreed. "Sadly true."

Before starting the car, she took her phone out again and opened the link to the view of Richard Morrisey. She'd never been in a position before where she'd actually been able to check up on what was happening to a victim. Normally, they were missing and she had no idea as to their location, or else they were already dead. Being able to log in and see exactly how he was doing was a novel experience. She wasn't one hundred percent sure she preferred it this way. Each time she logged in, her heart was in her throat, beating too fast and hard, and she half expected to find the victim already dead.

If she felt that way, she couldn't imagine how hard this must be for Richard Morrisey's family and friends. Word about what was happening was bound to spread. Nancy Morrisey was going to need guidance and support regarding what to do about handling this with her family, and also the media.

How many people were watching the video now? She checked the number of views, which was also on a counter beneath the video. It had crossed the twenty thousand mark and was adding more with every passing minute. How big could this thing get?

She thought of something. "Maybe the reason the kidnapper hasn't demanded anything yet is because they're waiting until they have what they consider to be the maximum number of viewers. Perhaps only then will they say what they want so they create the biggest impact?"

"I think you're onto something. Do you think Daniel Southern was right when he said this could be politically motivated?"

She pressed her lips together and nodded. "It's definitely something to consider. Maybe they've decided this will create more impact than supergluing themselves to something."

"Maybe, but it's a hell of a risk to take. I mean, you can't do serious time for gluing yourself to something, but you can for kidnapping and holding someone against their will."

"Or worse, if it comes to that."

"We'll find him first," Shawn assured her.

She hoped he was right.

Half an hour later, Erica pulled up in front of a three-storey, Georgian Grade II listed townhouse. It wasn't far off one of the garden squares, and she was sure the place would be worth millions. Again, the possibility that this was happening because of money went through her head. These people were clearly well off, and if the kidnapper knew where they lived, that the children went to private school, and what Nancy did as a job, they'd know that, too. But if this was all about money, why put on the whole charade with the video? Yes, it might be creating an impact, but so would Richard going missing accompanied by some photographs of him being held prisoner.

Erica climbed out of the car and reached into her pocket for the keys Nancy had given her. That Nancy had been more than willing to hand over her house keys to the police could mean that she had nothing to do with what was happening to her husband. It could also mean that she was simply confident the police wouldn't find anything there to incriminate her.

She went to the boot and opened it to remove some protective outerwear. She handed a set to Shawn.

This was a potential crime scene now.

"I assume that's Richard's car," Shawn said, nodding at the silver Mercedes-Benz GLE in the driveway. It was a luxury 4x4 and was probably worth six figures new.

Erica checked her notes for Richard's licence plate number. It was a match.

"He must have driven back here after he delivered the children to school. Let's find out if he made it into the house."

She rang the bell and waited. When she got no response, she hammered her fist on the door. Around her, she sensed curtains twitching. In a neighbourhood like this, the arrival of the cops was bound to garner some attention. Not that she cared. All the neighbours would be receiving visits from them very soon to find out if they'd seen anything.

"Police," she called. "Anyone home?"

There was still the possibility the video was a fake. If Richard Morrisey opened the door, wondering what all the fuss was about, they'd know they were wasting their time.

She gave it a moment, and when there was no reply, she put the key in the lock and slowly opened the door.

"Police," she called again. "Is anyone here?"

The house had that distinct atmosphere of emptiness, and Erica relaxed a fraction. She edged deeper into the Morriseys' property. On a hall console, a letter had been opened. She picked it up and checked the date. "Written yesterday, so he must have opened it this morning. What time does the postman deliver around here? If he opened it when he got back, we know he made it home."

Shawn nodded. "I'll ask around."

Together, they moved through the house. The first door to the left led onto a large living room, and the one on the right was a study, the walls lined with bookshelves. Each room was dominated by a huge fireplace, and the real wood flooring was scattered with expensive rugs. She spotted a large, framed photograph of Nancy and Richard on their wedding day, looking at least ten years younger, and beaming at the camera. He seemed very different to the broken man chained to the chair.

Shawn had already headed into the rear of the house, where an immaculate kitchen with an extension that included bifold doors out onto the garden was located.

"Erica," he called back to her. "Come see this."

She tore her gaze from the photograph and went to join him. She found him standing over a stool that lay sideways on the floor.

"It isn't much as far as signs of violence goes," he said, "but it's something."

She agreed. "Looks to me as though it should have been standing up here at the breakfast bar." She indicated to where three other stools were positioned, all upright. "Maybe Richard was sitting here, and he was caught by surprise. Someone grabbed him from behind, perhaps, or knocked him unconscious, and he fell from the stool." She studied the area around the item of furniture. "I can't see any blood, but someone might have cleaned it up."

"And leave the stool lying on its side?" Shawn said. "What would be the point, especially since they haven't exactly tried to hide the fact he's been abducted. I mean, they're streaming it online."

"Good point. Let's get SOCO in, see what they can find."

It made sense that this was the place he'd been taken from. What was the point of entry? Any signs of a struggle?

"We need to go door to door, speak to all of his neighbours, find out if anyone saw anything. Ask if any of them have CCTV or doorbell cameras. Let's get a record of what cars are on the street, make sure we can identify them all."

"Whoever took Richard must have had transport," Shawn said. "He's not a small man. If someone took him from his home at nine in the morning, someone must have seen something."

"I think if anyone saw a grown man being hauled from their house, they would have called nine-nine-nine."

Erica spotted an iPhone sitting on the kitchen counter beside the kettle. With one gloved hand, she picked up the phone.

"It's switched off," she said.

She took an evidence bag from her pocket. The phone would be useful. It might help them confirm what they already knew—that Richard left the house to take the children to school and then returned here. If they could find out what time the phone reconnected to the house's Wi-Fi, then they'd have an exact time when he came back. The built-in satnav on the car would also help confirm that, but it wouldn't give them an exact time to tell them when he'd been taken, which was what they really needed to know.

Her heart went out to the children. They weren't even teenagers yet. Plenty of people would be unsympathetic and say kids of that age should be kept away from social media, but Erica knew from experience that it wasn't as easy as it sounded. The schools all expected homework or homeschooling to be done on iPads or computers, and they needed to be on Wi-Fi to work. It was impossible to watch them twenty-four-seven. The hardest part was that the kids seemed to know their way around the internet and apps even better than the adults, learning how to hide things from a parent's prying eyes.

The local newspapers and reporters would be getting their claws into this soon enough, too, and then it'd be everywhere. It was impossible to shelter children completely. Their friends would hear about it, and they'd gossip just as much as the parents. She remembered when her husband had been murdered, and how hard the fallout had been. Poppy had only been small then, and she hadn't really understood everything that had happened—thank goodness—but the Morrisey children were old enough to understand.

"What's out the back?" she asked.

The walled garden was long and narrow and perfectly manicured. But there were only other gardens on all sides, and no way out. She'd thought if there was a gate that led onto an alleyway, or something similar, whoever had taken Richard might have used that as an entry and exit route, but she couldn't see them hauling him over a six-feet-high wall.

She shook her head, twisting her lips. "They must have used the front door, which meant they brought him right out into the street. How did that not attract any attention?"

"Could Richard have gone with them willingly?"

"It's something to consider."

She spotted something attached to the wall of the house facing the rear garden.

"Those are security cameras." She left the back garden and went to the front of the house where the same cameras were positioned near the front door. At a glance, they seemed to be working, too. "Why didn't Nancy Morrisey mention that they had cameras?" Erica wondered out loud.

"She was in shock. It probably didn't occur to her. We should have been the ones who asked."

"You're right. Let's get in touch with her again, see if she can send us the footage."

They were the types of cameras that linked up to an app on a phone and stored the footage online for a monthly fee. With any luck, the Morriseys paid that fee and they'd have captured exactly what had happened on camera. The rise in home use of security cameras might not sit comfortably with everyone, but they definitely made an investigation easier. Nothing stood up in court like actual video footage of a crime being committed.

If the footage was good, it was a hard thing to argue your way out of.

Erica placed a call to Daniel Southern. "How's she holding up?"

His voice came down the line. "Still shaken but keeping it together. The children are both with us now, too, so they'll all be taken to a safe location."

"Good." She jumped in with her reason to call. "We're at the house now and noticed there are security cameras. Can you find out if Mrs Morrisey has access to the footage, and if so, can she send it over to me. My email address is on the card I left for her."

"You think the abduction was caught on camera?" he asked.

"We'll know more when we see the footage."

"I'll get it sent to you ASAP."

"Thanks." She ended the call.

Shawn had requested reinforcements, so they stayed at the scene until uniformed officers showed up, together with SOCO.

He ran the sergeant through what they knew so far and what needed to happen with the scene.

"We're going to need all the neighbours interviewed to find out if anyone saw anything. Let's get forensics on the car as well. There's a possibility Richard picked someone up on his way back from dropping the children at school. Maybe he even knows the person who took him. He might have even gone with them willingly for all we know."

"You're taking this seriously, then?" the police sergeant asked Shawn. "It isn't some kind of a prank?"

"Right now, it looks real. Let's hope it does turn out to be a prank, though, because it'll mean an innocent man's life isn't in danger."

Chapter Six

Erica and Shawn left the crime scene in the hands of SOCO and the uniformed officers. They grabbed a very late lunch, eating in the car so as not to waste any time, and returned to the office.

Erica called a briefing with the rest of her team.

As well as Shawn, DCs Jon Howard and Hannah Rudd were both present, as were a number of others who'd got wind of the video online and wanted to find out more. DCI Gibbs also sat in on the briefing, taking up a standing position at the back of the room.

A map of the area around Richard's home and the route to his children's school had been pinned to the incident board, together with some screengrabs that had been taken from the livestream. Also included were recent photographs of both Nancy and Richard Morrisey.

Erica got started. "This is possibly one of the strangest cases I've come up against, and right now, I'm still not completely sure what to make of it. It would appear Richard Morrisey, the husband of a Minster of State, Nancy Morrisey, has been snatched from his home sometime after nine a.m. and is now chained to a chair in a room, current location unknown. We know this because his ordeal is being livestreamed online for anyone who wishes to view the footage."

Erica took a couple of paces across the front of the room. "It's possible the motive for the kidnapping is political, but they're also a wealthy family, so it may be financial. No demands have been made yet, that we're aware of. Nancy

Morrisey has her own security team who have been to the children's school and pulled them out for their own safety. We don't yet know if Nancy or the children will also be at risk, but until we can be assured of that, they've been taken to an undisclosed safe location. We are still able to speak to Nancy, and we have requested access to the video footage from the security cameras at her home.

"We believe Richard was taken from his home sometime shortly after arriving back from dropping his children at school, but it is possible he was taken earlier, and the scene was set up to make it appear as though he was taken after arriving home. Our last current proof of life was here," she pointed to the map, "at the private school his children attend, but hopefully we'll pick him up on CCTV sometime during his commute home as well. The livestream of the incident began some time before eleven this morning, which means, if our timings are correct, wherever Richard is being held must be within approximately an hour and a half's drive of his home. Unfortunately, that doesn't help us narrow it down too much." She considered something. "How fast does London traffic move at that time in the morning?"

"It's not fast," Shawn said, "but even at ten miles per hour, that still gives us a large search radius, since we have no idea which direction he was taken."

Erica agreed. "Yes, but at least it's something. Scenes of Crime Officers are at the Morriseys' house right now, so hopefully they'll be able to find us something more to go on. The only sign of a disturbance was a stool knocked over." She indicated a photograph that had been taken at the scene.

"Not exactly a bloodbath, is it?" Jon commented. "Plus, he doesn't look injured in the videos."

Hannah twisted in her seat to address her colleague. "No, but they disabled him somehow. A grown man would fight back if he found someone in his home and none of the rest of his family was there. There doesn't appear to be any signs of a fight."

Erica nodded her agreement. "They might have moved fast, possibly even drugged him. We weren't able to see any signs of forced entry at the property, so perhaps whoever did this may have had access to a key or was known to Richard. Richard may have opened the door and invited this person in, and they then caught Richard by surprise." Erica moved on. "We do have uniformed officers going door to door with the neighbours to find out if anyone saw or heard anything."

Erica had had a computer brought in on a wheeled trolley, like the kind she remembered from school that the teachers used whenever they'd wanted to play a film instead of actually teaching the class.

She turned on the monitor, and the livestream of Richard Morrisey played onscreen. A ripple of unease went across the room, though they'd all seen the footage already. But there was something unnerving about working an investigation when it was possible to look directly at the victim in real time.

"When the footage began," she said, "the clock was started at sixty-seven hours and forty-three minutes, and is counting down. To what? We don't yet know, but let's hope it's not the worst possible outcome."

"Is it possible that the clock starting at sixty-seven hours is significant in some way?" Hannah Rudd suggested.

"It's possible. It's a little under three days. Maybe that means something. Whoever is behind this must have chosen that length of time for a reason."

Around the room, heads were nodding and thoughts and ideas scribbled in notepads.

"Since he's been imprisoned," Erica said, "Richard has been trying to communicate with the camera, though unfortunately it doesn't look as though he's aware the police might be watching. With any luck, it'll occur to him that he can also tell us what he remembers about the events leading to him waking in that chair."

"Do you think he knows how many people are watching?" Jon asked.

"I doubt it, but the voice at the start informed him that he has an audience, so he knows someone is watching."

Erica paused to take a drink of water. Her mouth had run dry from all the talking.

"There are going to be three lines to this investigation. The first is learning about Richard Morrisey's final movements, and Richard and his family in general. Has someone been stalking or threatening them? Do they have any financial issues they don't want us to know about? Is there any kind of discord in the marriage? The second is studying the space he is in—what can we see or hear that'll help us narrow down his location? The third is the online presence, the technical task of finding out IP addresses and trying to learn where the feed is coming from." She nodded over to where Karl Hartley was sitting near the back of the room. "We have Digital Forensics working on that."

Karl cleared his throat. "So far, it appears as though they're using a sophisticated VPN to hide their location. It's pretty much what I'd expect. It's going to take some time to crack it."

"Time is one thing we might not have," Erica said. "Keep me updated as to any progress made."

"Will do."

She looked to one of her constables. "Jon, can you get hold of any traffic cam footage from around the area at the time we believe Richard was taken. Run plates and see if any of them flag up warning signs. Whoever took Richard must have moved him from his home to whatever location they have him at now, and they didn't carry him there which means they used transport of some kind. They don't live out in the sticks. There are plenty of surveillance cameras around, and I'm one hundred percent sure that we'll have caught the vehicle they used on at least one of those cameras. We just need to figure out which ones."

"No problem," Jon said.

"Let's see if we've got traffic cameras en route to the school as well," she added. "Try and capture Richard while he was driving. Check if he was alone. Maybe someone was following him."

Jon nodded. "Good idea. They might have been wanting to make sure he kept to his regular routine and didn't decide to stop off for coffee with someone or have an appointment somewhere."

Erica was half thinking out loud now, her mind whirring with ideas. "Hannah, can you get in touch with the school, ask some more questions. I assume they'll have their own security footage. Also find out what Richard's final movements were.

Did he get out of the car with the children when he dropped them off? Did he stop and speak to anyone? What kind of mood was he in? Let's ask the right questions."

Hannah scribbled everything down. "On it."

"We've got Richard's mobile phone, which has also been sent to Digital Forensics. Shawn, can you request bank and phone records. Maybe he stopped for fuel or groceries on his way home and used his card. Who did he last speak to and who's he been messaging. Maybe Richard was aware that someone was stalking him? Perhaps he's received threatening messages but had kept it to himself so as not to worry his wife. Let's find out if his wife knows the code to get access to the phone."

Shawn made a suggestion. "If these people are good with technology, they might have even accessed Richard's phone themselves. All it would take is for Richard to have clicked on a bad link to give them access to it. Maybe they were able to retrieve his calendar, so they knew exactly where he planned on being on any given day. If they were capable of everything else, they'd be capable of that."

"Good point."

Erica rounded things off and made sure her team knew what their actions were. With any luck, they'd get the footage from the security cameras any minute now—she was surprised it hadn't arrived already, considering Nancy Morrisey understood how urgent it was. They might also hear from the uniformed officers going door to door that they had a witness to Richard's abduction.

She grabbed a fresh coffee and returned to her desk.

A message arrived on her computer. Nancy had sent the security footage, but with it was the note, 'I don't understand what this is.'

"Shit," Erica muttered to herself.

That didn't sound good.

She downloaded the footage and then hit play. She narrowed her eyes and leaned forward, as though getting a better view could change what she was watching.

"What the hell?"

Had Nancy sent her the right file?

The video had the narrow viewpoint of security footage, but it wasn't of the Morriseys' property. It was from a neighbourhood in a far more rural area—in fact, Erica didn't even think it was anywhere in the UK. The homes opposite the position of the security camera were all wooden structures. Brown water ran past like a river, carrying with it tree branches and numerous other unidentifiable objects.

She continued to watch. At nine-fifteen, the video footage of the flooding ended and switched back to the correct footage of the Morriseys' driveway, Richard's Mercedes still in the position they'd seen it in.

Erica watched it for a moment and then dragged the video back to before the footage had been interfered with. At eight fifty-two, the image of the driveway vanished and was replaced by the floodwater.

"Well, I guess this gives us a solid timeframe within which Richard Morrisey was taken," she said to herself.

She got on the phone, dialling the number she had for Daniel Southern, who would act as the go-between to try to keep Nancy's location a secret. "Have you watched the footage?" she asked him.

"Yes, I checked it myself," he said. "Someone must have overridden the footage shot during the time Richard was taken and put this in its place."

"Why do that? If they had access to the security footage, why not just wipe it?"

"Honestly, I have no idea."

"Is someone trying to send us a message?"

Daniel answered with a question of his own. "Any idea where the recording was taken?"

"It's impossible to tell. I can get Digital Forensics to take a look at it, but from what we can see it's a place where the buildings are wooden and that's suffered a flood fairly recently."

"Why fairly recently?" he asked.

"Because this kind of technology has only become widely available in the past few years, and at a price that someone who'd live in a neighbourhood like this would be able to afford."

"Those are all excellent points," he said, "but it could still be anywhere. Besides, it might not even mean anything. The footage could have been selected at random."

"Give me a minute."

With the phone clamped between her ear and shoulder, she ran a reverse video search on the output.

"Nothing's coming up online," she told him. "Wherever they've taken this footage from, it's not just a random video grab from the internet. I think this is something they've taken personally, or that someone has sent them. And in the meantime, we don't have the security footage from the

Morriseys' house, something that would have been of great help to us, so my guess is this has been done deliberately."

Daniel huffed out a breath. "That's not good news. Hopefully one of the neighbours' houses will have cameras and caught something."

She sat back, disappointed. "Yes, let's hope so."

Right now, they had no idea where Richard Morrisey was, or who had taken him.

Chapter Seven

To say he was uncomfortable wouldn't even be a hint at how Richard felt.

The chair had turned into a torture device. His back screamed from sitting bolt upright for so long, and no matter how much he tried to slouch or twist, or bend forwards, it didn't help. His fingers were freezing cold, and numb, apart from the occasional bout of pins and needles. He wished he'd allowed himself to put on more weight, because now the bones of his arse seemed to have zero padding and were becoming bonier by the hour, digging into the solid wood of the chair.

He'd fallen asleep a couple of times, his eyes growing heavy, his head bobbing, but he didn't dare give in to the rest. What if something happened to him while he was sleeping?

How many hours had he been in here now? With no windows, and after falling asleep, it was impossible to tell.

"What do you want from me?" he cried at the camera. "Just tell me what you want, and I'll do it."

He waited for a moment, half expecting to get a reply from the person who'd first spoken to him, but there was nothing.

"Money?" he tried. "Is it money you're after? Because if it is, I can work with that. My family is wealthy, as I'm sure you already know. Contact my wife and name your price. She'll make sure you get what you want, and then you can let me go, okay?"

He pictured a faceless man, lurking somewhere in the dark, beyond the floodlights, watching and waiting. Richard had never been imaginative as a child. He'd never been one of those boys who'd believed in monsters lurking beneath the bed. But now his imagination conjured the worst kind of monsters—human ones—ones who planned something very bad for him indeed.

He'd been holding back his emotions, but only silence greeted him, and he lost control.

"Fuck!" he screamed. "What the fuck do you want? If you don't want money, tell me what you do want!"

Still, no reply came, and Richard barked out a sob. He dropped his chin to his chest, his shoulders shaking.

It wouldn't be until no one picked the children up from school that anyone would even realise something was wrong. He had no appointments that day, nothing that he would be missed at. Maybe Nancy would try to call him, but she wouldn't worry if she wasn't able to reach him. She'd simply assume he was busy, and she'd have too much going on herself to even give it a second thought. He pictured the kids at the end of school, standing with their teacher, wondering why their dad hadn't shown up. The school were bound to call him then, and, when he didn't answer, they'd try Nancy. Maybe then she would remember that she hadn't been able to get hold of him earlier in the day, and that would be the start of it dawning on her that something was wrong.

He stared at the camera. A red light continued to blink, indicating it was working. What was it in here for? The voice had told him to say hello to his viewers, but what did he mean by that? What viewers? It definitely sounded as though there was more than one, so did that mean the man had a partner or a colleague who'd also helped to bring him here? Or was he talking about a different group of viewers entirely? Maybe this was some sick video for perverts who got off on people in distress?

Nothing would surprise him these days. The world seemed to be becoming a more and more fucked-up place. He worried about what kind of world the kids would grow up in, what sort of hate and perversion they'd be exposed to in their lives.

From somewhere behind him, the trickle of water running grew louder. It had never sounded like a tap, more like a broken pipe, maybe. Suddenly, however, it had more force, as though someone had opened a stopcock.

He frowned and tried to twist his head to get some idea of what was happening. Was the water coming from a burst pipe behind a wall?

Something cold and wet touched his already chilled bare toes. He glanced down to find water gathering, turning the grey concrete a shade darker. It snaked past him, running off into some unseen corner at first, but then seemed to grow heavier, pooling around his feet. He couldn't even do much to keep his feet dry. While he could lift them a couple of inches, that was the farthest the chains would allow, and pretty soon his thigh muscles and abdominals trembled with the strain.

Fuck. It must be a burst pipe.

Where was the door? It must be beyond the glare of the floodlights that half blinded him. Beyond them was only darkness, and it was a darkness that was hidden from him by the lights. There must be some form of entry, as he'd been brought in here, as had all the equipment. Had someone blocked it up again? Why would they do that? It wasn't as though he was going to escape anytime soon. He was chained to this chair, and the chair was bolted to the floor. He wasn't going anywhere.

"Hey!" he shouted. "There's water coming in here. I think there's a leak somewhere. You need to help me."

Still, no one replied.

Help wasn't coming.

What would happen if the water got faster? Or even if it stayed at this amount, and there was no sign of him being let out of here? What if it had nowhere to go and it gradually started to creep up, covering his feet and then his shins and then his knees and chest? He would drown in here, strapped to this goddamned chair.

Another thing occurred to him. The camera and the lighting had power running to them, and now there was water on the floor. Richard raised his feet again. It wasn't far—a few inches at most. If the water got to any kind of depth, he might risk being electrocuted.

He took in the camera and the lighting. Both had been placed on tall tripods, which had then been attached to the floor. It didn't look as though there was any electric cables snaking across the floor, but because of the lighting, his vision was obscured. The electrical cables would be connected to the backs of the equipment, not the stands. So as long as the water didn't get too high, he might be all right.

How high would it get, though? It was still coming and didn't seem to be showing any signs of stopping. The flow of the water was slow and steady, but still frightening. He pictured himself chin-deep in the water, with it threatening to rise above his head. Being chained to the chair meant he wouldn't even be able to swim.

Panic overwhelmed him once more. He forced himself to take some deep breaths. Panicking wouldn't save him, and it wouldn't help either. It wasn't easy, though, and it simmered beneath the surface.

Think, Richard. Think.

The water was making him even colder than he already was. Why was it so cold in here? His whole body vibrated with it, his muscles trying to keep him warm. There must be something he could do.

His gaze was drawn back to the camera again. He had viewers, didn't he? The voice had told him so.

He locked his focus on the camera, staring straight into it, and addressed whoever was beyond.

His voice trembled as much as his body, but he pressed on.

"Please, I don't know if anyone can hear me, but I'm trapped in here, and now there's water coming in. I don't think it has anywhere to go because it's rising. If it keeps rising, and I can't get out of this chair, then I'm going to drown. My name is Richard Morrisey, and I'm married to Nancy Morrisey. We have two children who don't deserve to lose their father this way. Please, if you're watching this, and you can do something to help me, then please do. I'm begging you."

He'd never felt so sorry for himself. His head hung as he sobbed, his shoulders shaking. What had he ever done to deserve this? Okay, maybe he hadn't exactly been a bleeding-heart liberal, but he'd given to charity on occasion, and had paid his taxes, and been a good citizen. He opened doors for old ladies and gave up seats for pregnant women. He'd been a good dad, at least he thought he had, and a decent enough husband. Maybe there had been a couple of times his eye had strayed, but he'd never followed it up with anything. He'd always done his best to support his wife in her career, even on the odd occasion when he felt like he was somehow less of a man for not being the main breadwinner and staying home with the kids instead.

An ache in his bladder alerted him that he needed a piss. He couldn't use his hands to unzip his fly and free himself. He was so cold. The urine would at least bring him some warmth. He didn't want to do it, but what else could he do? It went against everything he'd been told since childhood, but finally his bladder released. Hot fluid—so hot against his chilled skin it almost burned—gushed down the inside of his thigh, pooling inside his jeans. It was blissfully warm, and for a moment he was grateful for it, but then, as it cooled, he realised he was going to need to sit in the urine now, wet and even colder than before.

Around him, the water continued to rise.

Chapter Eight

Not long after she'd got off the phone with Daniel Southern, Shawn approached her desk.

"There's been a development with Richard," Shawn said. "Have you seen it?"

"I haven't checked recently. What's going on?"

"Water is coming into the room. It's already at Richard's knees. It must have been there earlier, but we didn't notice it because of the angle of the camera."

"How quickly is it rising?"

"At a guess, from what we've seen so far, about a foot an hour, possibly more."

Erica frowned. "How tall is Richard when he's sitting down?"

"He's five feet ten standing, but it's harder to tell how tall he is sitting down. It's not as though when someone is sitting they're exactly half their standing size. It varies depending on the individual's body proportions and the way they sit, plus how tall the chair is."

"Okay, let's assume sitting he's about eighty percent of his standing height." Erica's brain threatened to short-wire. Maths had never been her strongest point. She'd barely scraped a pass at GCSE. "That's what...fifty-six inches, approximately. How long are we looking at before the water level reaches his nose and mouth?"

Shawn's forehead creased as he thought. "Only a couple of hours from now," he guessed.

"But if he's due to drown in another couple of hours, what's the point in the countdown timer? Because according to that, he's still got more than sixty-one hours left."

He shook his head. "Honestly, I don't know. Maybe the countdown is to something else. If Daniel Southern is right, and this is politically motivated, it could be counting down to an attack of some kind."

She let out a breath and scrubbed her hand over her mouth. "You could be right, but I'm not sure. This feels more personal for some reason."

Shawn didn't have the answers any more than she did.

The link to Richard's livestream was already open on a tab on her computer, so she clicked it open. Sure enough, water swilled around Richard's knees. Understandably, he seemed distressed by this new development and was trying to escape, only to be brought up short by the chains around his wrists and ankles.

Erica had to admit the footage was morbidly fascinating. She could understand why so many people were glued to their screens, watching Richard's situation unfold. It was incredible how quickly word had spread about what was happening, and even though they'd put out a social media blast requesting people not to watch it, and asking them to respect the victim's privacy, it had probably had the opposite effect in actually pointing people in the direction of the livestream. They hadn't linked to it, of course, but it didn't take people much in the way of searching to find it.

Was Richard going to drown, right in front of everyone?

"That water doesn't look clean," she observed.

"No, it doesn't. It's not coming from a tap or hosepipe then?"

"I guess not. Does that mean wherever Richard is, he's near a water source? That might help us narrow down where he might have been taken."

"There are water sources all over the city."

She huffed out a long breath. "I know, but we've got to work with what little we've got right now."

"Which isn't much at all."

Erica thought for a few seconds, tapping her pen against her lips. "One thing I don't understand is why we haven't heard anything from the kidnapper. What is his goal? His motive? If it was money, wouldn't we have heard something by now?"

"I think we need to dig into Richard's connections more, the wife's connections as well. Have they had any run-ins with anyone? Any arguments? If money isn't the motive for what's happening, then maybe it's revenge?"

She looked up at him. "You think someone might be punishing Richard?"

"Or his family," he said.

"If someone is trying to prove a point, why aren't they telling us what it is?"

"I'm not sure. Maybe they're waiting for something to happen that we're not aware of yet."

Jon interrupted them. "Boss, I think I've found something. A plate doesn't quite match up to our records."

"Let's see," Erica said.

"It's been altered. It's for this van. I've just sent you the image."

She clicked off the footage of Richard and pulled up an image of a white van with a company logo on the side. It was blurry, and Erica squinted at it.

"What business is that?"

"A commercial laundry business, at least that's what it's disguised as, but I checked the name with Company's House, and there's no such business registered."

Erica considered this. "It would be a good way of getting someone in and out of a house without being seen."

"You think they might have opened the back of the van," Shawn said, "rolled out a commercial laundry cart, gone into the house with it, and rolled Richard back out in it?"

Jon nodded his agreement. "If they covered him with a sheet, no one would be any the wiser. I bet plenty of these residents have cleaning and laundry businesses come to their homes. It wouldn't have attracted anyone's attention."

Erica looked between both men. "I think you're probably onto something. Do you think we're dealing with more than one person?"

Shawn nodded. "Makes sense. Moving those commercial laundry carts around isn't exactly easy. Now imagine it with the weight of a full-grown man inside. It's only a hunch, but either it's more than one person, or we're dealing with someone who has the strength of an ox. Say he knocked Richard unconscious...he'd then have needed to lift Richard up and into the cart. That would have taken some effort if it was just one man, but could be handled easily if it's two. My guess is they'd want this to be done quickly, in and out, so they wouldn't want to stand around, wrestling with Richard's unconscious body to get him in there."

"How far can we track the van?" she asked.

"I'm still working on that," Jon said.

"Okay, we need to be on the lookout for that plate and the vehicle description."

Her phone rang. It was Daniel Southern again, and he didn't sound happy.

"Are you watching this?" he snapped. "What the actual fuck is happening? Are you any closer to finding him? Mrs Morrisey is beside herself, thinking she's about to watch her husband drown, together with hundreds of thousands of complete strangers on the internet."

"We're still working on tracking the location, but we have a possible lead on a van that might have been used to transport him. Whoever is behind this hasn't made it easy for us, but we're doing everything we can."

"You're running out of time, Detective."

"I'm very aware of that, but we're dealing with professionals here. Someone's covered their tracks at every turn."

"The water is still rising, and it's not showing any signs of slowing down."

"Like I said, we're doing everything we can, but unless you've got something helpful to tell me, I'm wasting precious time by being on the phone to you."

"Fine."

He ended the call.

Erica covered her face with her hands and tried not to scream.

Pushing Daniel Southern out of her mind, she focused on the van, and researching the company name it had advertised.

Even if the company wasn't real, they must have had the sign professionally made. Was there any way they could figure out who made it? Was there anything on it that said what sign producing company it came from?

It wouldn't be easy to track down, however. It could have been ordered online, and God-only-knew how many companies there were out there who made signs, but it might give them a solid lead, something they were desperately missing right now.

Time moved by swiftly—too swiftly.

Tearing her from her research, the landline on her desk rang with an internal call. It was the front desk.

"DI Swift, I have someone from the Counter Terrorist Unit here to see you."

Damn. This must be because of Nancy Morrisey's job.

"I'll be right there."

Erica hung up and then went to the front desk.

The woman waiting for Erica was in her fifties, in a beige suit, her thin brown hair pulled into a ponytail. She spotted Erica and approached, her low-heeled shoes clacking on the floor, her hand outstretched. The woman's thin lips didn't so much as quirk in a smile as their hands met and they shook.

"DI Swift," Erica introduced herself.

"Tina Werner," she replied, "from the Counter Terrorist Unit. Where can we talk?"

"Through here," Erica said, leading her through the office and into the briefing room.

"I assume you've already realised I'm here because of what's happening to Richard Morrisey?"

"Yes. Is this to be considered a terrorist attack?" Erica asked.

Tina didn't sit but instead turned to the board where everything they'd learned so far had been pinned. She spoke, her back to Erica.

"It's something we have to consider. Our politicians have been murdered in the past by Islamic State sympathisers. We don't know that someone with the same beliefs isn't behind this, too."

"What makes you think it could be politically motivated?"

Tina Werner faced her. "Nancy Morrisey's voting record on UK airstrikes in Syria could well be motive enough to give them a reason to kidnap her husband, as is her membership with a Friends of Israel group. It wouldn't be the first time."

"Politicians have also been murdered by far-right groups. Why jump to Islamic State sympathisers?"

"The streaming of the footage online. We've seen them use similar tactics with the beheading of victims by Islamist extremists. It's a way of creating propaganda and instilling shock and terror into the general public. Wouldn't you agree that this is exactly what this video of Richard Morrisey is doing?"

"No one has been beheaded," she pointed out.

She was aware of how these extremist groups used live beheadings to terrorise people and streamed them online. There had been campaigns to try and get the social media sites to remove them, but the sites had said they'd keep them as long as they were shown in a negative fashion, not as propaganda. In Erica's mind, that was nowhere near good enough. How must the poor victim's families feel, to not only see something so horrific happening to their loved one, but also knowing that footage was available online for millions of others to view over and over again? The thought of it was unbearable.

"Not yet, they haven't." Tina's words were ominous.

"Why haven't they claimed to be the ones responsible? If someone wants to be feared, then they have to let us know who they are in order for that to happen. Currently, no one is claiming responsibility for kidnapping Richard Morrisey."

Tina folded her arms across her chest. "That doesn't mean they won't. This all could be building up to something."

"Do you know of any groups who have connections with laundry companies?" Erica pushed a grainy printed photograph across the table. "This is an image caught by CCTV of the van we believe may have been used to transport Richard. We haven't been able to find any record of the company, but perhaps it's something you've come across before?"

Tina stared down at the picture and shook her head. "It doesn't ring any bells, but I'll ask around. I'm sure you're aware that we have people of interest who we are keeping a close eye on. I'll make enquiries to see if any of them have altered their patterns of behaviour recently or if any have disappeared off the radar altogether. We'll monitor online chatter as well. There might be code words that are being used."

"There's also the possibility this has nothing to do with an extremist group," Erica said, "and we'll receive a demand for a ransom from the kidnapper very soon."

"I don't get the sense that this is a ransom situation. Ransoms are normally done quietly. They don't want anyone else to know. In fact, that's often one of the main conditions they stipulate is that the person they send the ransom note to doesn't tell anyone else. This is too public. Someone is trying to make a point."

Erica couldn't argue about that.

"Until we know for sure what the motive is for Mr Morrisey's abduction, we'd like to work side by side with you. More hands, and all that."

"Agreed. Will you be able to help try to track the origin of the video feed?"

"Of course. We'll get our best people on it."

Erica had the feeling Counter Terrorism would have more powerful computers and a team trained in this kind of thing, but she worried that they'd be too focused on their assumption of there being Islamist extremists at the root of this that they'd blind themselves to any other possibilities. She was glad they hadn't pulled the case out from under her, though. The only reason she could think of for them not taking the case from her was that they weren't one hundred percent sure who was behind this either.

She saw Tina out, and then Shawn joined her.

"Looks like they've brought the big guns in," he said.

"It's because of the livestreaming. They think it could be Islamic extremists. Nancy's voting record apparently might be enough for them to turn on her husband."

"What do you think?"

"I think they'd have claimed responsibility by now if they were behind this."

Shawn nodded. "I think you're right, but Counter Terrorism will have more information than us. Maybe they got wind of something like this happening before it did, which is why they've jumped in."

"Perhaps, though I wish they'd stopped it before it happened, if that's the case. The family, especially the children, don't deserve to go through this."

For the next couple of hours, Erica got back to work, but it was impossible not to be distracted by the volume of water that was now in the room with him. Her team were gathering around, all of them watching on with horror.

"What about the electrical equipment?" Hannah said. "There must be a power source or they wouldn't be able to have lights or run the camera. What if he doesn't drown but he ends up electrocuted instead?"

A murmur of worry rippled around the office. It was a perfectly valid point.

Jon made a suggestion. "Maybe they're attached to the ceiling. The vantage point does seem high up. That way, the water won't touch them."

Because the camera was pointing towards Richard, they weren't able to see the setup themselves.

"That makes sense," Erica agreed. "If someone wants this to be seen by thousands, if not millions, of people online, they're not going to risk the lights or camera being short-circuited by the water."

They were all glued to the screen. The water was up to Richard's neck now. Much higher, and he was going to have to tilt his head back to keep his chin, mouth, and nose above water.

"I think it's started to go down," one of the team members in the office shouted. "It's not getting any higher."

Was that true? Internally, Erica prayed they were right. She sat focused on the screen, watching the water level intently. Sure enough, it appeared to be going back down.

Richard had a reprieve, at least for the moment.

All around the office, the team exhaled a collective breath of relief.

Chapter Nine

Jasmin Webb sat back in her gamer's chair.

Like most of the population right now, she was fascinated by the scene that was unfolding on the internet. The man chained to the chair. The timer counting down. Him almost drowning.

She fingered the braids knotted close to her scalp. She'd only had them done a few days ago, and they were still too tight, pulling uncomfortably. It wasn't ideal, but there was no way she was wearing her hair natural. It was far too much work. The discomfort did keep her awake, but it wasn't as though she ever slept anyway. Maybe the energy drinks she was addicted to didn't help with that, but she wasn't giving those up anytime soon either.

In the comments on the livestream, everyone was speculating about what was going on, but it looked real to her.

<Anxiety is at an all-time level watching this – but I can't seem to look away!>

<If you like crazy videos, subscribe to Fiction Fact>

<Where's the humanity? People need to stop watching this shit – if it's even real.>

Even the local police had left a comment, asking anyone who had any more information to get in touch via a special helpline. Jas didn't think she'd like to be the one in charge of that helpline. The number of bullshit calls they'd be receiving must be huge. There were already hundreds of comments on the video, and that was only going up by the second. The more shares the video got, the more the content would spread like wildfire.

Jasmin thought the video was real. There weren't any of the usual signs she'd watch out for to tell if this had been created by a deep fake AI, but it was possible. AI was improving every single day. Even so, she found herself studying the screen for all of the tell-tale signs. As good as the technology was, there were still things it couldn't seem to get quite right, such as details like human fingers or eyes. There was always something a little off about them. But in this case, the man onscreen appeared as real as any other.

A shout came from upstairs. "Jas, come and get your dinner."

Jas let out a sigh and sat back, her head tipping towards her spine. She'd already told her mother she wasn't hungry, and yet her mum still insisted on making dinner for her. Most of her friends' families ate later in the evening, around seven or eight, but her mother insisted on eating early because, according to her, it wasn't good to sleep on a full stomach. In Jas's mind, all it made her do was eat two dinners, because she was always starving again by bedtime.

There was no point in trying to argue with her, though. Her mum would always win at the end of the day.

Jasmin dragged herself up the stairs. Their flat was upside down, with the front entrance at street level and the bedrooms and bathroom downstairs in the basement.

She must admit, the food did smell good, the air redolent with allspice and ginger.

"Ah, there you are," her mum said when she caught sight of her. "I thought you had those damned headphones on again and didn't hear me."

"I heard you," Jas said. "With your set of lungs, I think half the street's coming for dinner."

Her mother laughed, taking the ribbing good-naturedly. "I think I've probably cooked enough to feed them all anyway."

Gloria Webb was what was known as a feeder. She only ever felt happy when she was cooking for others and then watching them eat.

"What have you got planned for this evening?" Gloria asked, spooning the chicken and sauce onto a bed of rice and sliding it onto the table for Jas.

Jas shrugged. "Same as normal. Nothing."

"I wish you'd go out and do some normal things girls of your age are doing. Shouldn't you be hanging out with friends, or maybe even dating? I'd like it if you had a boyfriend."

"They're all dumb. All they want to talk about is sports or video games. It's like they have no other interests."

"All you want to talk about is computer stuff. Isn't that exactly the same?"

Jas was nineteen years old now and really needed to move out, but prices in North London, where she lived, were insane. Even the tiniest one-bedroom studio was well over a grand a month, and she couldn't afford that. She considered finding a house share, but the thought of living with a whole heap of people she didn't know made her shudder. What would they make of her computer setup? There was no way she could move out without taking her computers with her. Would they be safe in a house share? What if one of the housemates decided to mess around with her stuff or brought someone dodgy back to the house while she was out and robbed her? It wasn't worth the risk.

Besides, she'd feel bad for leaving her mother all alone. Since her dad had died, it had only been the two of them. Sure, Gloria had her own friends, but that wasn't the same as family. And yes, maybe she would miss her mother, too.

Jas knew she had it good. All her meals were bought and cooked for her, all her laundry was done, the place kept tidy. Jas did try to help out when she could, but she didn't often think about it. It simply didn't occur to her. She'd get involved in a project online and lose hours, if not days, before she lifted her head again.

If only some of these gigs actually made her some real money.

She tried not to think about an offer that she'd been made recently. It would be illegal, but it would mean she'd have some money. Big money. And there was very little chance of it ever being traced back to her. She told herself it was a victimless crime. Only the big banks would pay for it.

Even so, she couldn't shake the guilt. It was the one thing that had stopped her saying yes. She worried that every time she used the money, or even looked at anything the money had bought, she'd be overwhelmed by the same sense of guilt. It wouldn't help her anxiety either. She was already conscious of how paranoid she felt all the time. Wouldn't she feel even worse if she was worried someone out there actually would be out to get her?

The people who'd made the offer were faceless names on the internet. She might do as they asked, but then what would she do if they didn't even pay her? It wasn't as though she could go to the police and put in a complaint. She had no recompense at all. What if she did it, and it was all for nothing? She was pretty sure it was a crime, even if she didn't get paid.

"Have you seen that video on the internet?" Jas asked, deliberately redirecting the subject away from her. She forked a piece of chicken, popped it in her mouth, and chewed and swallowed. "The one with the man in the chair."

"That can't be real, Jasmin. It's a fake, surely?" Even her mother had a smart phone, though she only used it for the basics.

"I'm not sure. It might be a publicity stunt or something, though it looks real enough to me."

"You don't think someone actually wants to hurt him, do you?"

"He already seems pretty distressed."

Gloria tutted and shook her head. "My God, that poor man. What is the world coming to? I'm sure the police are doing everything they can to find him, assuming it is even real."

"There's a clock counting down to something," Jas commented. "The time of his death, maybe."

Gloria's fork paused on the way to her mouth. "You can't be serious? No one is going to kill someone live on the internet."

"It happens all the time, Mum."

Her already big eyes went even rounder. "I hope you haven't been watching anything like that."

"I am an adult. I can watch what I like."

"Not under my roof, you can't."

"Okay, Mum," she said, just to placate her. It wasn't as though her mother would have any idea what Jas was watching. Jas could clear her search history in seconds.

The truth was, she'd go downstairs the moment she'd finished her food and bring up the online footage of the man again.

That shit was getting addictive.

Chapter Ten

Erica felt guilty leaving work when they still hadn't located Richard Morrisey, but she couldn't be too late home that evening. It was Poppy's last night before she left for her residential, and Erica wanted to make sure they'd packed everything on the kit list and that they got to spend the evening together.

She grabbed a pizza on the way home and went to pick Poppy up from her sister's house.

Natasha answered the door. "Hi. Come in for a minute."

Erica stepped inside the house with her. "Is everything all right? Is Poppy okay?"

"Yes, she's fine. I just wanted to talk to you about something."

Erica frowned. "Then talk."

Natasha glanced towards the stairs, to make sure no little ears were nearby, and lowered her voice. "I assume you know all about this video that's going around? The one with the man in the chair?"

"Yeah, it's somehow become my case."

Natasha's eyebrows lifted. "Oh my God. It's real then? There's so much speculation online about what's actually happening, it's hard to know for sure what's the truth."

"We believe it's real. The man in the video is missing, and there are signs of a disturbance at his home."

"That's terrible. His poor family. I can't imagine having to watch someone I love going through such a thing. What absolute bastards would do something like that to a person? Are you any closer to finding him?"

"We've got people working on it overnight. We don't think he's been taken far as the recording started not long after we believe he went missing, but since we don't know what direction he went in, it's still a needle in the haystack right now."

"Does the person who took him intend for him to drown?"

"Honestly, Natasha, we simply don't know what their motives are. If it wasn't for this being Poppy's last night at home, I'd still be at the office myself."

She felt guilty for leaving—an emotion she was becoming more than familiar with. Though she trusted her team, and everyone else she worked with, a part of her still felt as though she'd abandoned Richard Morrisey to die. Was there anything more they could be doing to try to find him? She thought they had all bases covered, and they'd narrowed down the search area, but they still didn't have any idea where he was.

"You're allowed to have a life," Natasha assured her. "You're a mother as well as a detective."

"I know, but the two roles aren't always easy to balance."

Movement at the top of the stairs drew her attention.

"Hi, Mum," Poppy said. "Are we going home now?"

Erica smiled at her daughter. "Yes, home time. I've got a pizza for dinner, and then we need to get an early night. Big day tomorrow. Say thank you to Aunty Tasha for looking after you."

Poppy came down the stairs, and Natasha unhooked Poppy's coat and bag from the stand by the door.

"Thanks, Aunty Tasha," Poppy parroted.

Natasha ruffled Poppy's hair. "Anytime, and have a fantastic time on your residential, okay? Don't go missing us all too much."

Poppy grinned. "I won't."

"Cheeky mare." Natasha laughed.

"Thanks again," Erica said.

They left Natasha's house and went back to the car. Poppy was big enough and old enough to strap herself in now, so Erica made sure she'd done it correctly and then slid behind the wheel.

During the drive home, Poppy chattered excitedly about the trip she was going on the following day. It was as though no matter how much she talked, she was never going to run out of words.

"I'm bouncing off the walls," she declared.

"Well, try to calm yourself down a little, because otherwise you're never going to sleep, and you don't want to be tired for your first day."

"I won't be. I'll be too excited then as well."

Erica laughed. "I hope your teachers have some idea about what they're getting themselves into. They'll be exhausted by the end of the week, dealing with thirty overexcited kids."

"Not everyone will be excited," Poppy said. "Alina won't be excited. Alina will probably cry. She cries at everything."

Erica pulled a face. "Oh dear. Poor Alina."

She signalled and turned the car into their street. As she drove closer, her stomach knotted, and her heart thudded. The road was looking distinctly busier than normal. Several cars were doubled parked around her house, and there were people lurking around as well.

Erica hesitated, unsure of what to do. Should she keep driving? Go back to Natasha's? But everything Poppy needed for her trip was inside the house, and she wasn't going to let these arseholes keep her away from her own home.

"Shit."

"You said a bad word, Mum," Poppy chirped from the backseat.

"Sorry, love. Do you see those people outside of the house?"

"Yeah. Who are they?"

"Reporters, and they're going to ask a lot of questions when we try to go inside, so promise me you won't say anything, okay?"

"Questions about that man online?"

Erica stiffened. "How do you know about that?"

"My cousins showed me."

Dammit. She should have checked with Natasha to make sure her kids weren't showing Poppy anything, but she'd been so busy, she hadn't even thought about it. Because Natasha's children were older, they didn't have the same kind of restrictions that Erica put on Poppy's online time.

There were several reporters around. She knew from experience that not all of them would be tied to specific papers. Some of them just freelanced and sold their stories to whoever was willing to buy them.

How did the press even find out she was the SIO on the case?

Erica stopped the car as close to the house as she could get it, since the reporters were blocking half the street.

"We're going to get out of the car," she told her daughter, "and go straight to the front door, without stopping to speak or even look at any of them, okay? Can you climb over to me, so we'll both get out of the driver's door." She didn't even want to be separated from her daughter for a second while Poppy climbed out of the back. These people were like locusts, and they wouldn't care that they were swarming all over a little girl. Erica intended on keeping Poppy as close as possible.

"Okay, Mum."

Poppy climbed over, and Erica took her hand.

"Ready? One, two, three...let's go."

She swung open the driver's door, almost hitting one of the reporters crowding around her. She kept Poppy's hand in hers, helping her scramble out of the car. With her other hand, she slammed the door shut behind her and locked it, not wanting to give the reporters a chance to rummage through her boot or glovebox in search of a titbit they could use in a story.

She kept her head down and marched to the house, doing her best to ignore the barrage of questions that were being flung in her direction. She released Poppy's hand to wrap her arm around her narrow shoulders instead, pulling her closer.

"DI Swift? Do you know where Richard Morrisey is being held yet?" one reporter shouted.

A second joined in. "This must be bringing back memories of when your husband was taken and held captive. What makes you think you can save Richard Morrisey when you weren't able to save your own husband?"

Every muscle in her body tensed, and she glanced down to Poppy. Her daughter stared up at her, her eyes wide, and Erica hugged her in tight, while continuing to propel her towards the front door.

She wanted to spin around and spit vitriol in the reporter's face, to tell him how shameful he should feel about bringing up a man's brutal murder in front of his young daughter, but she knew it would do no good. Anything she said would be twisted and used against her just to create a sensational headline. She didn't care what they said about her, but it was her instinct to protect Poppy.

They reached the front door, and she opened it and bundled Poppy inside. She shut the door on the reporters, then she went around closing all the curtains and making sure all the windows and doors were locked. She doubted any of them would resort to breaking in, but it still made her feel safer.

She found Poppy still standing in the hallway.

"Why is that man chained to the chair?" the girl asked.

"Honestly, love, we're not really sure."

"Is it because he's married to someone important? Like Daddy was with you?"

"I'm not really anyone important."

"But you were to the man who hurt Dad."

"Yes, I guess I was..." Erica's thoughts lingered on Poppy's comment. Was that what this was about? The person who'd taken Richard wasn't punishing Richard at all, but instead was trying to hurt Nancy?

She kissed her daughter on the head. "You're a clever girl."

Erica's stomach rumbled, and she realised they'd left the pizza on the back seat. "Oh, damn it."

"Mum!" Poppy exclaimed once more.

"Sorry, sorry. I left the pizza in the car, and I don't want to have to go back out there to get it."

"It's okay. We can have cereal."

"Yeah? You sure?"

"I like cereal."

Erica appreciated how understanding her daughter was being. Plenty of children her age would be throwing a temper tantrum about now, demanding the pizza they'd been looking forward to. But Poppy accepted the change in circumstances easily. It hadn't even upset her that they needed to fight their way through the reporters or what one of them had said about her dad. Sometimes, Erica worried about what kind of lasting effect her job would have on her daughter. She wondered if Poppy would ever want to join the police force, or if her experiences with her mother had put her off for life. Erica didn't mind either way. All she wanted was for her daughter to be happy. She didn't want her to go through the trauma of this job, but, at the same time, Erica was aware that being a detective was where she got her self-fulfilment from. It made her feel like an important member of society—that she had a reason to exist other than being a mother or a sister.

"Let's eat," Erica said, forcing a smile and trying to forget about the people outside, "and then make sure you've got everything for the morning, then we'll get a good night's sleep. We've both got a big day tomorrow."

Chapter Eleven

The following morning, Erica took her daughter to where the coach waited outside of school to take the children on their residential. All around them, parents had gathered at the coach, ready to wave off their offspring.

The first thing Erica had done that morning was bring up the feed to make sure Richard Morrisey was still alive. She'd woken several times during the night to turn on her phone, checking he was okay. Though she'd been sure someone would have phoned her if he'd died, she still couldn't help but worry about him.

The second thing she'd done was see if anyone had contacted her with developments overnight. The third thing was to make sure the damned reporters had gone, which they had.

The clock was still counting down, and the number of viewers had exploded, as had the comments.

She couldn't imagine how uncomfortable Richard must be feeling. Not only was he still chained to the chair, which must have been killing him by now, he was also soaking wet. During the night, the water level had risen again and then gone back down. He shook violently, probably a combination of shock and the cold. Had he believed he'd been about to die? If the people watching had thought exactly that, then she was sure he'd believed the same.

She helped Poppy into the huge backpack they'd bought specially for the occasion, settling the straps around her shoulders. The children all needed to prove they could carry their own bags by taking them to the coach to be loaded onboard. The teachers wouldn't want to be carrying thirty different bags when they got the other end.

They'd been given a list of items to bring by the school, but that hadn't stopped Poppy adding to it. As well as the multiple t-shirts and leggings and pairs of socks, plus waterproofs, pyjamas, jumpers, and a change of shoes, Poppy had also insisted on bringing several books, two of her teddies, and a small pink fluffy cushion that she liked to use as a pillow. Then there were all the snacks she'd claimed they needed, plus a lunchbox and water bottle for the journey.

The way Poppy was loaded up, she could be a gap-year student heading off on a year backpacking around South-East Asia instead of a primary school child going on a residential trip for a few days.

Erica observed her daughter in the huge backpack. "If you fall over in that thing, you're going to be like a turtle lying on its back, arms and legs waving in the air."

"What do you mean, Mum?"

"You're not going to be able to get yourself back up again."

Poppy laughed. "I'm sure someone will help me, or else I'll just have to make sure I don't fall over."

"I think not falling over is probably the best way to go."

"I hope I don't have to sit next to Lilly on the coach. She always tells the teacher about everything."

"How about you simply don't do anything that needs to be told about."

Poppy rolled her eyes. "You mean have no fun."

"No, I mean you behave yourself."

Erica knew she'd got lucky with Poppy. She was a good kid—especially after everything she'd been through. She at least in part had her sister to thank for that—after all, Natasha and her family had helped to raise Poppy—but she also liked to think she'd played a hand in it.

"Are you going to miss me?" she said, pulling her daughter in for a hug.

"Yes, I'll miss you."

"I bet you won't. You'll be too busy having fun with your friends."

Erica kissed the top of her silky-soft hair and squeezed her tighter. It was only for three nights, and it wasn't as though Poppy hadn't been away without her before. It was always hard knowing your child wasn't home, though, that they were miles away and you weren't nearby if they needed you.

Erica hated the way her mind catastrophised things, but she thought anyone who'd lived through the sort of things she had, who saw day in, day out what could go wrong for people, how evil people could be to each other, that they'd do the same.

All the possibilities of what might happen to Poppy while she wasn't under her watch ran through her head. One of the people who worked at the centre might have a thing for young girls. Someone in charge of the abseiling might have a drink problem and not have checked the equipment correctly. The driver of the coach might have a heart attack and veer across the motorway and crash.

Erica's head wasn't always a fun place to live.

"If you get lonely," Erica said, "check the inside pocket of your bag."

"Why? What's in there?"

"Just a little something for you. But only open one a night, okay?"

Erica had written Poppy a little note for each day of the trip, telling her how much she loved her, and how proud she was of her, and how she couldn't wait to see her. Maybe it was soppy, but as there wouldn't be any kind of communication, except for in an emergency, while the children were away, it made Erica feel as though Poppy would still get to hear her mother's voice each day, even if it was only in her head.

"Is it money?" Poppy asked, her eyes bright.

Now it was Erica's turn to roll her eyes. "No, it's not money, cheeky."

Poppy giggled.

She would be absolutely fine, Erica realised. This was probably harder on her than it was on Poppy. Poppy would have her friends and the activities as a distraction, while Erica was home alone.

She did have this case, however, and she was sure that would take up plenty of her time. It had been almost twenty-four hours now since the live feed had been playing, and they were no closer to finding Richard Morrisey or working out who had taken him. The water had been worrying, but at least he was still alive. A part of her had been concerned that she was going to check in next time only to find a body, though she was fairly sure she would hear if someone had killed him. She wasn't the only one glued to what was happening online. According to the counter, there were over a million viewers now. The numbers had exploded overnight as the rest of the world clocked on to what was happening. What did this person want? Whoever had taken Richard hadn't yet made any demands, but someone didn't pull off something like this without a motive. Unless they were sick in the head and simply playing games, but there was something too organised, too deliberate, about it in Erica's mind.

"Time to go," the teacher called over the tops of children's babbling, excited voices, and some teary parents. "If everyone can line up, we'll get both the bags and the children loaded up."

She would wait until Poppy and the other children were all safely on board and then she'd wave them off. She hovered, anxiously aware that she also needed to get into the office. Finally, they were ready to set off, and she smiled and waved with the other parents as the driver gave a toot of his horn, and then they were gone.

Feeling strangely deflated, Erica went back to her car. She opened the door and got in, settling herself behind the wheel.

Her phone buzzed. It was a text from Shawn containing a link. She never clicked on links that didn't come from what she thought might be an untrustworthy source. There were so many scams around these days, all it took was a single click on a bad link, and people could access phones or laptops remotely, getting into bank accounts and credit cards, or taking over your social media. Erica did her best not to have anything like that on her phone. She didn't trust the banking apps, and social media was her idea of hell—too many people trying to outdo each other to show off their best lives to make others jealous.

This was Shawn—who she literally trusted with her life—but she still wanted to make sure it was safe.

Quickly, she typed a message back.

What's the link to?

Instead of getting another message in return, her phone rang. She answered it. "Morning."

Shawn jumped straight in. "I think we've got another one. I don't know how to explain it. It's best you watch it for yourself. That's what the link is to."

"Shit. Okay. Give me a second."

Erica clicked on the link and braced herself. What was she going to see?

Onscreen, a glass door appeared, through which the camera appeared to be recording. Behind the glass door was a wooden panelled room, with yet more wooden benches positioned across the back and side of the walls.

Inside the room was a woman.

She appeared to be in her forties. She was slim and wore a white shirt and a grey trouser suit. Her face was flushed, her hairline damp with sweat. She lifted her hand and banged on the glass, her mouth opening where she was clearly shouting, though, as the audience, they were unable to hear her. It didn't need to be audible for them to know what she was saying, however.

The poor woman was clearly shouting for help.

Like with Richard's livestream, there was a countdown clock in the corner of the screen. The number showed forty-five hours and thirty-one minutes. It was the same time as on Richard's screen, except, Erica assumed, the new victim's clock had only recently been started.

Erica put the phone back to her ear. "Who is she?"

"I have no idea," Shawn said.

"The speaker hasn't said her name at all?"

"Not yet."

"Is she another politician, or related to a politician?" Erica asked.

"I don't recognise her, but that doesn't mean she isn't. Any idea about the room she's in?"

She was surprised he didn't recognise it.

"It's a sauna. She's trapped in a sauna."

"Jesus. What's the kidnapper trying to do? Roast her to death?"

Erica shuddered at the thought. What a terrible way to die. She thought she'd prefer Richard's way of drowning, though drowning while being chained to a chair, while having your death livestreamed to millions, wasn't exactly pleasant.

"God, that poor woman," she said, unable to tear her eyes from the screen. "I can't imagine what she's going through. I can't stand being in them for more than a few minutes, and even that makes me feel claustrophobic. The fear of being trapped inside one is very real."

"She's not going to be helping herself by banging and screaming like that either. She's only going to make herself hotter and waste whatever fluid she has inside her. Does she have any water in there with her?"

"Yes, there's a bucket in the corner. I think you're supposed to use the water to tip over the coals to make it hotter in there, or create more steam or something, but she's not going to be doing that."

"Hopefully, she'll have the sense to use it to hydrate herself while we figure out how the hell to get her out of there," Shawn said.

A pause came down the line while they both considered the immensity of the task. They didn't even know who she was, never mind how to find her.

"Could this just be a coincidence?" she suggested. "An accident? Maybe it doesn't have anything to do with whoever took Richard?"

"It's not. He's deliberately linked to it in Richard's livestream and directed people here. Plus there's the clock. That's not an accident."

She wanted to make sure they covered all bases before they jumped to assumptions. "How do we know the same person is responsible and we're not looking at some kind of copycat?"

"Honestly, we don't, but would someone be able to pull this off in such a short time frame? Setting up the equipment would take time, never mind selecting and kidnapping a victim. Plus, according to Digital Forensics, the setup with the VPNs is the same. How would someone who isn't connected to this know the exact way they've been broadcasting the live feed?"

She sat back in the driver's seat. "You're right. That would be unlikely."

"Hang on," Shawn said. "Something's happening. Watch Richard's feed."

Quickly, she took the phone away from her ear and switched the video feed to go back to the one of Richard.

He was in much the same position as before, except now a voice was coming over the speakers.

"Now we've hit one million viewers, it's time we revealed the next part to our plan. We've posted a link to a second video below. Please, can everyone follow the link."

There was a pause, and then the same message repeated over again.

Richard sat up straight, staring around, clearly trying to figure out where the voice was coming from.

Erica put the phone back to her ear. "If only there was a way we could communicate with him. He might be able to tell us something that could help us find him. Maybe he remembers something from when he was taken, an address or a description. Anything could help."

"But how? Short of taking over whatever equipment is being used to do that voiceover, it's impossible."

She let out a sigh and rubbed her hand across her face. "I know, but maybe we'll think of something. I'm coming into the office now. Can you gather everyone in the incident room and brief them on this latest development? I'll have to contact Tina in Counter Terrorism, too, see if she thinks this is still linked to an extremist group."

"Do you think she might be right?"

"Honestly, Shawn, I don't know what to think right now."

Chapter Twelve

E rica drove into the office as fast as she dared. As she'd expected, several reporters lurked outside. She'd been relieved that morning when she'd got up and discovered they'd abandoned her front door, but it looked as though they'd found a new location to hang out at.

She parked her car, braced herself, then threw open the door and climbed out.

The reporters sprang to life when they saw her and threw a barrage of questions in her direction, all shouting over the top of one another to be heard. She was aware of photographs being taken, but she kept her head up and walked straight to the entrance of the building. She hadn't done anything wrong and refused to be shamed by them.

"Detective Swift, who is the woman in the latest video?"

"Do you know where Richard Morrisey is being held yet?"

"Do you think he's going to die before you find him?"

She didn't answer any of their questions but paused briefly to respond.

"There will be an official press release later today," she said and kept going.

She reached her office and shook her head. "Jesus Christ, damned vultures."

Shawn joined her, pushing a black coffee into her hand as she headed for her desk.

"We're going to need to tell them something," he said. "Every man and his dog are speculating over what's going on."

"As are we. It's not as though we have anything more substantial to tell them."

"No, but saying something as simple as that we've identified the victims and are working to free them might be enough to keep them happy for the time being."

She stopped walking. "Except we haven't identified the victims. We don't know who the woman is."

"No, we don't, but we will. I'm sure of it."

She'd never seen the briefing room as full as it was today. Everyone who was connected to the case was there, including a representative from Nancy Morrisey's security team, Karl Hartley from Digital Forensics, and her boss, DCI Gibbs. There was also Tina from the Counter Terrorism Unit, though Erica hadn't had the chance to contact her yet. She'd clearly found out from her own sources. People were shoulder to shoulder, and they jostled over chairs. It was a strange atmosphere, almost an overexcited buzz, while everyone was trying to suppress it.

"Good morning, everyone. I'm sure most of you are aware by now that as well as Richard Morrisey, we have a second victim. She is currently unidentified, but it would seem she's been taken by the same perpetrator or perpetrators as Richard. Like with Richard, she has a countdown clock. It would seem they're both counting down to the same time."

Normally, she'd have scene-of-crime photographs and post-mortem reports, but all they had was Richard's address, the description of the van, and the strange security footage.

But one thing they did have was the live footage of the victims. It was on a split screen on the computer—one side showing Richard, still in the chair, and the other, the currently unidentified female victim in the sauna.

On the video, the female victim was still screaming. She'd pounded her fists against the glass so hard that she'd broken the skin, and now streaks of blood marred their view of her. Erica wished she could tell the other woman to calm down, to try to relax. She was only going to make the situation worse for herself by getting herself worked up and even more overheated. It was easier said than done.

Eventually, the woman onscreen gave up and sank to the floor, her legs folded beneath her, her forehead pressed to the foggy glass. Utter despair and helplessness radiated from the victim.

Erica couldn't imagine how terrified and uncomfortable the woman must be feeling. Did she have any idea that she was on camera? The abductor had announced to Richard to say hello to his viewers. Would he do something similar with this woman?

"Our priority needs to be finding out her identity," Erica continued. "Let's contact misper and see if there have been any reports of a woman matching her description going missing. Are we able to get a good enough image of her face through the glass to see if we can get any matches with a facial recognition search?"

"Yeah, we're already on it," Karl Hartley said.

"Good. That'll be a start. Please tell me you've been able to find out where this livestream is coming from?"

"We can't get a hit on the IP address. It's fully encrypted. Normally, we'd be able to hack it, but this is a clever one. They're using a form of virtual private network, but it's set to reroute every few minutes. So one minute their web traffic can be routed through a Canadian server, and the next minute their activity is showing as being through a German server. It's like falling down a rabbit warren."

Erica turned to Tina. "What about your guys? Any better luck?"

Tina shook her head. "I'm afraid not, but we're working on it."

"Can we get the livestreams shut down?" Erica asked them both.

Karl pursed his lips. "The danger with that is we might lose the link altogether, and we won't know what's happening with the victims, and we'll also be risking not being able to trace it at all."

Erica understood, but it didn't ease her frustration. "We need to work faster. We haven't got any time to waste."

"Maybe we need to look at bringing in outside help," Shawn suggested. "Like a hacker. Someone who knows how to crack codes."

"I'm sure Karl can handle this," she said. "Right, Karl?"

Karl nodded. "I'll certainly try my best."

"Do whatever you can, and the rest of us will work on finding the victims the old-fashioned way." She turned her attention to the rest of the team. "From the new video footage, it would appear the second victim has been trapped in a sauna. Until we find out who she is and what her last movements were, it's impossible to know where that sauna is located. We could attempt to contact all the saunas in the country, but that's going to be in the thousands. Every swimming pool has a spa pool and sauna included these days. Every hotel in the country probably has one."

"She has to be somewhere private," Hannah said. "If she was in a hotel or public spa right now, other people would be around. Plus, if whoever has taken her is expecting to keep her captive for two days, they're not going to want to be interrupted."

Jon gestured at the screen. "And how do we even know the livestream is coming from this country? If we look to Scandinavia, every home in the country has one."

Erica nodded. "Agreed. Attempting to check all the saunas is a needle in a haystack. We need to narrow down the search. There must be something on the video that'll help us. Are there any identifying numbers anywhere—on the thermometer, or engraved into the wood? What about scrutinising the glass in the door for any reflection of the camera or anything else that might be in the area we can't see. We need to zoom in to get more detail. What about the victim? If the facial recognition software doesn't pull up anything, we might need to go to the public and ask for their help. Do a social media appeal and see if anyone might recognise her, maybe even see if the press will help."

"You don't think that'll be fanning the fire?" Tina Werner said. "If we resort to social media or the press, someone is bound to post the link to the video and drive traffic towards it."

Erica pressed her lips together as she considered this. "You're right, but we don't have much time. If the countdown clock is to be believed, she has less than two days to live."

Tina angled her head. "Assuming that's what the clocks are counting down to. We're not aware of any chatter about a different kind of attack happening within the next two days, but that doesn't mean it isn't possible."

Shawn joined in. "If the clocks *are* counting down to their deaths, how can whoever is behind this predict when they're going to die? The sort of stress they're being put through could easily give someone a heart attack. Plus, we don't know if this victim has any underlying health issues. While she might appear to be physically fit, she could have high blood pressure, or a weak heart, or suffer from asthma. Any of those things might be fatal at any minute if the temperature gets much hotter in there."

Erica turned to stare at the screen again. "We don't even know where she is, never mind how we can get her out." She sensed the hopelessness of the case threatening to drag her down and quickly shook herself out of it. There was still plenty they could do to find the victims before it was too late.

"What about the voice?" she said. "The one that comes over the speaker? Is there anything we can do with that?"

"I can try to isolate it," Karl said, "and then use AI to compare it to all the other voices on the internet. I can't say how well it's going to work, though. It might come back with nothing, or it might come back with a thousand hits. There's no way of knowing until I try."

Erica nodded her approval. "Then try. Even something as simple as narrowing down an accent so we can figure out where they come from will be a help."

"Got it."

"How are we getting on with Richard's phone records and his bank details?"

"We've been able to trace all the numbers to people he knows," Shawn said. "There aren't any threatening messages on there or anything like that. The bank records don't show anything abnormal either. Healthy balance, no unusual deposits or withdrawals or transfers. Nothing that raises any red flags."

"Maybe this thing *is* political then," she mused.

Across the room, several heads nodded in agreement.

Erica moved on. "I'm sure you're all aware by now that we have CCTV footage of the van we believe Richard Morrisey was transported in. Unfortunately, the plates are fake, and it's safe to say so is the company. We're still circulating a description of the vehicle to see if anyone recognises it, or the company name. It might jolt someone's memory." She took a breath. "Also, I've been in touch with the sergeant running the crime scene at Richard's house. We have one neighbour who lives across the street from the Morrisey house who says they noticed the van belonging to the laundry company parked on the street, but that's all."

"What time did the neighbour say they saw it?" Hannah asked.

"Shortly after nine, which fits in with our timings, too. No one else saw or heard anything. What about the school? How did you get on there?"

Hannah crossed her legs and leaned forwards slightly. "Nothing abnormal to report. Richard got out of the car and walked the children to the gate and said goodbye to them there. As far as we can tell, he went straight home. There's no indication that anyone was following him."

Each way they turned seemed to be a dead end.

Erica rounded up the briefing, making sure everyone knew what they needed to be doing. Her nerves were frayed, and it was only early. She didn't like feeling out of control of a situation.

Shawn caught up with her. "I think I might know someone who can help with tracing the IP address."

"You do? Who?"

"Her name is Jasmin Webb. She's actually a relative of mine. A distant cousin. I haven't seen her for years, but even when she was younger, she was always incredible with computers. She hacked into the National Cyber Security Centre at the age of fourteen, got into a lot of trouble for it."

Erica lifted her eyebrows. "I'm not surprised. How old is she now?"

"Nineteen or twenty, I think."

"She's young, and a civilian. I'm not sure we'd even get clearance for her, especially if she has a past record."

"She was a juvenile then."

She shook her head slowly. "I'm still not sure. There must be someone else."

"Every minute that passes, the lower the number on the countdown clocks get."

"Surely there must be someone else," Erica said. "Someone in government security who'd be better for the job?"

Shawn sucked on his teeth. "People in government security are expected to toe the line. The way this person is working isn't within the realms of what's right and wrong. We might need someone who'll be willing to break some rules and knows how to do it."

"I don't know, Shawn. It doesn't sound like a good idea to me. We might need someone, but not a civilian. Let me ask around, see if we can find someone more suitable."

He clearly didn't agree with her, but he gave her a rueful smile. "You're the boss."

Chapter Thirteen

Hannah Rudd approached Erica's desk, a sense of excitement and urgency radiating from her. Before she'd even reached Erica, she blurted, "I think I've found out who the female victim is."

"Tell me," Erica said.

"Her name is Catherine Taura, and she's forty-two years old. She works for a company called Offshore Solutions Limited. High up, too, from what I can tell."

The younger detective handed a photograph over to Erica. It appeared to be one that had been professionally taken, perhaps to go on a website or an ID badge. The woman in the photograph had expensively cut dark hair in a sleek bob, and perfectly discreet makeup. She seemed to have little in common with the terrified person in the sauna, but it was definitely her, or else her twin.

"Is she local?" Erica asked.

"Yes, her most recent address is in Greenwich, but she works in the city where the company have their head office located."

"Anyone report her missing?" she asked.

Hannah shook her head. "Not yet."

"Is she married? Does she have children?"

"She's married, but no children."

"Does she have any kind of record?"

Hannah pursed her lips. "Clean as a whistle."

From her photograph, she didn't look like someone who got in trouble with the law.

"Have her next of kin been informed?" Erica asked.

"I've asked uniformed officers to go and speak to her husband. The fact he hasn't contacted us himself tells me that he has no idea what's happened to his wife, so it's going to come as a shock."

"Unless he's involved," Erica suggested. "Or we have the wrong person. We'll need to speak with him ourselves. Do we know when she was last seen?"

Hannah glanced down at her notes. "From the small amount of digging I've done so far, it would seem the security guard at the parking garage below her building saw her arrive first thing this morning, but she never made it up to her office."

Erica considered this for a moment. "Somewhere like that will have cameras. It might give us something to go on."

"That's what I'm hoping. I've requested the footage. The security guard says she didn't come back out again, at least not that he saw, and the car is still parked in the same spot."

"How many vehicles came in and out during the time between her entering and then the videos being broadcast?"

"I've no idea, but the footage can help us with that. There's a good chance she was in one of the cars leaving, even if the security guard didn't see her."

Erica got to her feet and called for the attention of the rest of the team.

"Everyone, we have an ID on victim number two." She repeated everything Hannah had told her. "I'm aware you're all still working to find Richard Morrisey, but I'm afraid I'm going to have to ask you to add a second layer to this investigation and inquire into Catherine Taura as well. It's going to be the same routine—tracking her final movements, getting any

CCTV footage that might be available, finding out if anyone had been following her, or if she received any strange calls or messages? Let's get her phone and bank records, see if we can pin down her final movements. The good news is she's local, and if she went missing first thing this morning, only for her livestream to appear not long after, it means she's being held within the vicinity of the city, just like Richard Morrisey."

"Does that mean both victims are being held at the same location?" Jon asked.

"Not necessarily. No one has been in to Richard this whole time, so it's possible they're at a different location with Catherine. It could be that they're delivering the victim to a location where the cameras are already set up and leaving them unguarded. Richard can't get to the camera because he's chained to the chair, and Catherine Taura can't reach it because she's locked on the other side of the glass door."

Jon nodded. "Makes sense."

"We should also find out more about Catherine, personally. Who are her friends and colleagues? How did she seem recently? Did she mention anything strange happening?"

"I can do that," Hannah said.

"Great, thanks. Any volunteers to come with me to check out Catherine's place of work and have a chat with the security guard, too?" She looked to Hannah again. "What's his name?"

"Arnold Fishgate," Hannah supplied.

Unsurprisingly, Shawn lifted his hand to volunteer. "I'll join you."

"Thanks. Let's go and pay Mr Fishgate a visit."

• • • •

WITHIN HALF AN HOUR, Erica found herself in front of the tall office block for Offshore Solutions Limited. It was an imposing modern, glass-and-steel structure that was at least twenty stories high.

The security guard's office was located at the bottom of the concrete ramp that led down to the below-ground car park. Parking was at a premium in central London, and she bet not everyone who worked in the building was rewarded with a space. How high up was Catherine to have her own spot?

The area where Catherine's car had been found parked had been cordoned off. A uniformed officer stood nearby. Until they knew what Catherine's final movements were, there was a good chance the car was a crime scene.

Arnold Fishgate was in his sixties. He was a short man with a combover, and a face full of crags that made him look older than he was. He kept glancing over his shoulder as though he expected the missing woman to emerge from the shadows of the underground car park.

"Mr Fishgate, I'm DI Swift, and this is DS Turner."

They both held up their IDs for the man to peer at.

"I'd like to ask you some questions about Catherine Taura."

"Yes, of course. I'm happy to help. That poor woman. I can't believe someone has done this to her."

"Did you know Catherine well?" Erica asked.

"Oh, no. Not at all. Only to say good morning to. Nothing more than that."

"Did anything unusual happen this morning, before or after Catherine arrived?"

He shook his head. "No, nothing. It was a normal morning, right up until I heard about the footage online, and then your lot got in touch."

"What time did Catherine arrive here at?"

"I've double-checked for you, and she got here at seven fifty-three this morning."

"How did she seem?"

He looked between the two detectives. "Fine. I mean, no different than normal. We didn't speak or anything, but she lifted her hand in a wave, and I opened the barrier, and she drove through."

"Did you notice if she stopped and spoke to anyone when she got out of the car?"

He pursed his lips, the lines around them deepening. "No, sorry. I wasn't really paying attention once she'd passed through the barrier."

"Did anyone arrive who wasn't accounted for? What about anyone in a white van?"

He frowned as he thought back. "Well...there was a catering company here. Said they were booked in for a breakfast meeting."

"Did you get the name of the company?"

"No, I didn't, but they must have arrived about seven-thirty and left again half an hour or so later."

"Did you check with whoever had booked them in?"

The man seemed to shrink, folding in on himself. "No, I didn't. I just opened the barrier for them."

"Did you get them to sign in? Anything like that?"

"I figured they'd do that at the reception desk, if they needed to. We have people coming and going all the time.

There would be a tailback if I quizzed every single driver. Do you think they might have had something to do with Mrs Taura being taken?"

"There was a white van linked to the previous disappearance, so it's possible, but then there are a lot of white vans in London, so it might be nothing."

He wrung his hands, clearly troubled. "I mean, how was I supposed to know something like this was going to happen?"

"It's okay, Mr Fishgate. This isn't your fault." She glanced over at Shawn. "We're going to need to find out if anyone in the building had catering booked for a breakfast meeting this morning."

"I'll get straight onto it." He left her to head into the building.

Erica turned her attention back to the security guard. "I need to see the CCTV footage, especially from where the van entered and left the location."

Had Catherine been in the back of it, unconscious or perhaps bound, with something over her mouth to prevent her shouting out for help? Or maybe she wasn't taken from the building or the car park. She might have got a call from someone asking her to meet them on foot somewhere, and she was snatched on the way.

"I've got access to it here," he said, "if you wanted to watch it now."

"We're going to need to get our technical people onto this," she said, "see if we can get some of the shots blown up. Can you get the footage emailed over to me, asap?"

"Of course."

"And I'd also like to watch it now."

He nodded and went to the computer to scroll back through the CCTV footage. "Where do you want to start?"

"How about when the white van arrives?"

"Sure thing."

He scrolled back until he reached the moment of the van driving down the concrete ramp and stopping at the barrier. There was a pause when Mr Fishgate asked the driver what his business was, and then the barrier opened, and the van passed though.

It was impossible to see either the driver or the passenger's faces. Not only was the angle bad, both were wearing branded baseball caps pulled down low. The driver's hands were on the steering wheel. She squinted at them. He wore a ring—perhaps some kind of gold signet. She'd get that blown up for a better view back in the office.

She turned her attention back to Mr Fishgate. "You must have got a look at the driver or the passenger?"

He glanced away, as though ashamed. "I wasn't really paying much attention, plus I forgot my glasses this morning. I left them at home on the kitchen table. I shouldn't really have even driven without them, but by the time I realised I'd forgotten them, I was already halfway here, and if I'd turned around and gone back, I'd have been late for my shift."

Damn it, Erica thought.

"There still must be something you can tell me. Any details might help. Age, colour, what accent he spoke with. Even the smallest thing might lead us to whoever has taken Catherine."

"I mean, they were both male, I can tell you that much, and both white, I think."

"You think? So they might not have been?"

He fluttered his hand around his head. "I'm getting on. My memory's not so good either."

So his eyesight isn't good, and his memory isn't good, Erica thought. Perhaps not the ideal person for a job that requires someone being vigilant.

"Any idea of their ages?"

"Not particularly young," he said, "but not old like me either."

"Middle-aged?" she prompted.

"I guess so."

She bit down on her frustration. If anyone else had been sitting in the security box when the van had driven in, they might have a semi-decent description of whoever might have taken Catherine by now, but instead, it was as though this man was being deliberately obtuse. Maybe he was? What if he was involved somehow? Perhaps they paid him to turn a blind eye?

She made a note to check into Arnold Fishgate. Maybe he had money worries that would make him susceptible to bribery.

She wished the angle of the camera had been slightly different so they could get a better view. She needed to find out what other cameras were in the building. Maybe they could get another angle.

"Excuse me, Mr Fishgate. I'm going to take a look around the rest of the parking garage. If you could email that footage to me asap, I'd appreciate it."

"Will do, Detective. Sorry I haven't been of more help."

Erica walked through the car park, to the spot where the van had been parked. The lighting was low, so she used the torch on her phone to study the area. They'd need to get forensics in here, see if they could get a tyre print. Was there anything else? Had they dropped anything, or had something fallen out of the van that might help the police figure out who they were?

She lifted her head to check the positions of the cameras. There weren't as many as she'd hoped, and there would definitely be blind spots. If the criminals were clever—which in this case she suspected they were—they'd have learned this information beforehand and taken steps to avoid being seen.

She approached Catherine's car—a sleek BMW Coupe. The uniformed officer guarding the scene nodded his hello, and she held up her ID for him to see.

"Any idea on how long it'll be before SOCO arrives?" she asked him.

"Shouldn't be too long. I'll make sure no one goes near the vehicle until then."

"I'm going to take a look."

"It's locked," he said, "and we don't have access to any keys."

That Catherine had taken the time to lock the vehicle indicated that she hadn't been dragged from the car. Erica pulled on gloves and shoe covers and ducked under the cordon. She peered through the windows of the vehicle, trying to spot any sign of trouble. Unlike her own car, the interior was spotless. No empty chocolate bar wrappers or bottles of water rolling around the footwell.

Catherine must have left her car before she was taken, so where was she snatched from?

Chapter Fourteen

Erica turned at the sound of footsteps approaching. A well-dressed man in his late fifties or so walked directly towards her. She ducked back out of the cordon and removed her gloves.

"Good morning," he said. "Your colleague said I could find you down here. I'm Robert Wheeler. I'm Catherine's boss here at Offshore Solutions."

They shook hands.

"Thank you for taking the time to speak to me," Erica said.

He pressed his lips together, nostrils flared, expression serious. "Of course. It's the least I can do when something so terrible is happening to one of our own. This whole thing seems completely insane."

"It's certainly...unusual. We've never come across anything like it—" She almost said 'outside of militant groups' but managed to clamp her lips shut. It wouldn't do any good to feed that kind of thinking into the general public.

She didn't want people to get it into their heads that this was any kind of radical group. Something so high profile would bring about people who wanted to take things into their own hands. If anyone suspected such a thing, there would be racially motivated hate crimes happening all over the city. Some people used any excuse to start trouble.

"Has Catherine experienced anything negative happening with her work recently? Has she mentioned having problems with anyone?" Erica asked.

He pursed his lips. "No, not that I'm aware of."

"What is it she does, exactly?"

"She heads up our strategy team."

"What does that involve?"

"She advocates for our business and works on creating a good profile for our company."

"Could she know Nancy Morrisey or perhaps Richard Morrisey through her job role?"

"The other person?" he checked. Then he thought for a moment. "It's possible their paths have crossed, yes. Nancy Morrisey is the Minister for Energy, and we're an energy company, so Catherine, or at least her team, have most likely worked with her at some point."

"Can you find out for sure for me? Have her secretary check her diary for any meetings that may have happened."

"Of course."

Erica made a mental note to ask Nancy Morrisey if she knew Catherine.

"Is there anyone else who Catherine was particularly close to who we might be able to speak with?"

"Her secretary, Martha. The two of them have always been tight. Catherine calls Martha her work mother."

"What about her real mother?" Erica asked.

"She passed a few years ago. I believe the only family Catherine has is her husband."

Erica wondered how her team were doing on following up with the husband.

She gestured at the ceilings. "Do you have a schematic indicating exactly where the security cameras are in the building that I could see?"

"I should be able to find you one. We've got CCTV cameras covering most of the garage, but not all of it."

"What about the stairwell leading up into the building."

"Yes, but not covering all of it."

"I'm going to need everything you have." She handed him her card. "If you can get it sent over to my email as soon as possible, I'd appreciate it. I'm sure you understand that time is not on our side. We've got footage of Catherine arriving at work this morning, but do you know if Catherine made it to her desk?"

"I'm afraid I don't remember seeing her. You'd be better off asking her secretary."

"That's Martha, right? Where can I find her?"

"In the office. Sixth floor."

"Thanks."

He gestured to the lift. "I'll ride up with you, show you where to go."

She took the lift up with him and allowed him to show her through the building to what was Catherine Taura's office. A woman in her sixties, and who was perhaps not far off retirement, sat at a desk positioned outside Catherine's door.

"Martha," Robert Wheeler said, "this is Detective Swift. She's investigating what's happened to Catherine."

The woman had her phone open at the video footage of Catherine. She raised her head and blinked back tears.

"I can't believe this is real. Who would do something like this to her?"

Erica was tempted to tell her to switch off the phone, but first she thought of something. "Can you look at Catherine's surroundings? Is there anything you recognise about it?"

The woman picked up her phone and frowned at the screen. "I mean, it's clearly a sauna that she's trapped inside."

"Do you know if Catherine ever used saunas?"

"Well, yes, of course she did. It's a good way to relax. Destresses the muscles, even better if it's combined with aromatherapy."

Erica wasn't interested in hearing all the merits of therapy. "Does Catherine have somewhere in particular she goes to?"

"Yes, a spa in Holborn. This isn't there, though. I've been there with her. This one is far too small."

Maybe someone saw her at the spa, Erica wondered. Could it have given them ideas?

The woman's chin trembled. "You've got no idea who's taken her then?"

"It's an ongoing investigation," Erica said, noncommittally.

"But Catherine has less than forty-three hours. You don't have much time to figure it out." Her voice rose in pitch as she spoke, betraying her inner panic. "How long can a person even survive in a sauna? Surely she doesn't have that long?"

"There's a possibility the sauna isn't heated, at least not to the temperatures we'd normally expect to see. She has time."

Erica wanted to say that they'd find Catherine before the clock ran out, but she couldn't make that promise. Right now, they had no idea who had taken either of the victims.

"And what about that poor man? The one in the chair with the water? You haven't found him either, so how do you think you're going to find Catherine?"

"We're working on it," Erica said.

She wished there was more she could do or say to offer reassurance, but the truth was that she didn't know if they were going to find either victim. She still didn't know what the kidnappers wanted. Normally, she'd have expected for there to be demands, but it felt like whoever was behind this was playing with them.

They clearly wanted a big audience, a desire to make an impact. They were clever, too. It was most likely going to be someone with a computer background, a programmer or hacker, perhaps.

Erica got to questioning Martha. "Did Catherine mention being worried about anything recently?"

"Like what?"

"Anything really. Whatever comes to mind."

Martha considered this for a moment. "I think she has the same worries as most of us. She has a big mortgage, so she was worried about money with the interest rates going up so steeply."

"She has money problems?" Erica checked.

"Not problems, no, but it's not cheap to live in London. Yes, she's on a good salary, but it's all relative, isn't it?"

"What about family or friends, or her husband? Any issues with those?"

"No, I don't think so, but she's a private person." Martha gave a teary smile. "She isn't one of those women who bitches about their husbands all day, every day. The two of them give each other plenty of space. It's always seemed to work between them."

"Does he work for the same company?"

Martha flapped a hand. "Oh gosh, no. I think he runs something to do with online training, but I honestly don't know much about it."

"Okay, thank you."

Erica still planned on speaking with Catherine's husband. Assuming he wasn't involved in any way, he must be frantic with worry about her.

Shawn joined her, and they both stepped away so they weren't overheard.

"I've asked every department in the building," Shawn said, "and no one ordered catering for a breakfast meeting."

"That van most likely was used to abduct Catherine then," she said.

"This is good news, right?" he said. "It means we have them on camera. Once we see the rest of the CCTV footage, we might even have the whole abduction."

"Yes, it is good news."

But though she'd said them, the words felt hollow. These people were clever. They'd have done everything they could to make sure their faces weren't captured and the van they'd used most likely had false plates.

"Would you give me a minute," she said. "I need to make a call."

She took out her phone and called Daniel Southern. "I need to ask Nancy a question. Is she there?"

"What's the question. I can ask her."

She exhaled a breath of irritation. "Just put her on the phone, please. I don't need to hear things secondhand."

"One minute."

"Yes?" Nancy's voice was sharp and full of tension.

"Do you know the name Catherine Taura?"

Nancy fell silent for a moment and then said, "No, I don't think so. Should I?"

"She works for Offshore Solutions Limited. It's an energy company."

"I'm aware of the company."

"And you're the Minster for Energy," Erica said. "There's a connection. Are you sure no one has been threatening you? No strange emails or phone calls?"

"They haven't kidnapped me, have they, Detective? It's my husband they've taken."

"Maybe to use as leverage to get you to do something for them," Erica suggested.

"No one has contacted me about anything except you." Her tone was brittle. "How much closer are you to finding my husband?"

"We're working on it."

"How? By worrying about business deals? This has nothing to do with Richard."

"Maybe not in your mind, but an outside observer could be thinking something else."

"This is crazy. I just want you to find my husband. Do you have any idea how tortuous it is to be able to watch him suffering like this? I've done my best to protect our children from seeing any of it, but when it's all over the internet and the news, how can they not see it? Even though I've stopped their access to the internet, they've got all their friends messaging them. They're asking me if their dad is going to die in less than forty-three hours."

Erica tightened her fingers around the phone. "I understand, Mrs Morrisey. Really, I do."

"How could you possibly understand?"

Erica took a breath. "I lost my husband to a crazed man, and I had to go through the same thing with my daughter, so I really do know what you're going through."

Her tone changed slightly, growing softer. "Oh, right. I see. I'm sorry to hear that."

"Thank you, and please understand that we really are doing everything we can."

Was it going to be enough? Like Nancy said, time was running out.

Chapter Fifteen

Before heading back to the office, Erica and Shawn grabbed a sandwich and a coffee.

She wondered how Poppy was getting on. She felt bad that she'd been so busy, she'd barely had the chance to give her daughter any more than a fleeting thought. The children would have long since arrived at the location of the residential and would probably already be out taking part in some kind of activity. Maybe it was good that she was so busy so that she wasn't moping around, missing her daughter.

They parked up to eat.

"I don't think we're going to have time for that dinner and cinema trip," Shawn commented right before taking a big bite of his sandwich.

"No, you're right, but we still need to eat?"

"Takeaway?" he suggested, just as she said the exact same thing.

"Great minds." She laughed. "Let's make it something spicy."

He pointed his sandwich at her. "You promise me you're not going to talk about the case all evening, though?

"I'm not going to make promises I can't keep. You realise all I basically have in my life is this job and Poppy."

"You have me, and you can talk about Poppy all you want."

"Thanks. I probably will since she's not here to talk about herself. Whenever she stays overnight with Tasha, the house is always so quiet. I don't know how she never runs out of something to say."

"I bet you were exactly the same as a kid," he said.

"Yeah, I was. I used to drive my dad mad. I think he switched off after a while and pretended like he was listening."

Shawn grinned. "Don't all dads do that?"

"I bet you wouldn't. You always seem to listen to Poppy, even when she's talking nonsense."

She caught his brown gaze in hers and stupidly found her cheeks growing warm. Had she implied he'd be a good dad—to whom? To Poppy, or to his own children?

That was another reason they couldn't work as a couple. He deserved to have children of his own, but there was no way Erica was going through the baby stage again. She didn't feel like she was mother enough to the child she had, never mind bringing more into the world.

Sensing the tension between them, she finished eating, started the car, and drove back to the office. She hoped the rest of the security footage would be waiting for her. Even with the security guard's poor description of the two men in the white van, it was still the best lead they had.

She got back to the office to discover the security footage from the office block had come in. She clicked play and watched it back with interest.

"Look at this," she called to Shawn.

He joined her at the computer.

Onscreen, Catherine was walking towards the stairwell door. She paused and glanced over her shoulder, as though she'd heard someone.

Erica willed that person to come into view.

Catherine stepped back, holding the door open, and a man, Erica assumed, from his tall height and broad build, wearing the branded catering baseball cap, and with a number of cardboard boxes stacked high and balanced against his chest, stepped into view.

Erica held her breath and willed the man to lift his chin, giving her a glimpse of his face, but it was as though he knew the camera was there and deliberately kept his head down. He used his chin to steady the boxes.

Where were the boxes now? Was the man wearing gloves? If they found them, they'd most likely be covered in the man's DNA. It wouldn't be much use if they didn't have something to compare it to, but it would still be something.

The man walked past Catherine, and she moved to follow him, allowing the door to swing shut. It didn't get the chance as the man blocked it with his body.

He acted swiftly, the boxes falling to the floor, all of them empty, and then grabbed Catherine in a headlock, choking her. It all happened so fast, there wasn't time for her to call out. Then he was manhandling her—presumably back to the van.

They were so lucky no one else had come along. At that time in the morning, plenty of people were coming and going, but they hadn't been interrupted. Admittedly, it had only taken a matter of seconds to actually abduct her, but they'd still got lucky.

A second man—who Erica assumed to be the passenger—ran over to pick up the dropped boxes. Damn. The chance of getting DNA or a print was minimal.

"What happened to Catherine's belongings?" Erica wondered. "Her handbag, her phone, her car keys? Have we got a trace on the phone? See if we can get a ping off a more recent location."

"I'll get onto it," Shawn said.

At least they had a general description of both men responsible now. The driver was definitely tall, with a muscular build, and was Caucasian. She also knew he wore a gold signet ring.

According to the security footage, only one man was in the van when they'd left the garage, but there had been two when they'd arrived. The passenger was most likely in the back with Catherine, keeping her quiet or making sure she didn't escape.

What did these people want? Why go through all of this? There was always a motive. It was very rare that people were kidnapped or killed for no reason.

Erica glanced up to find Hannah Rudd leading an attractive but red-eyed man through the office, towards her desk.

"DI Swift," Hannah said, "this is Catherine Taura's husband, John."

Erica rose from her desk to shake his hand. "I'm so sorry for what you and your family are going through right now."

"Thank you. I honestly can't even believe this is real. Who would do such a terrible thing?"

"That's what we're trying to find out. I understand this is distressing, but do you mind if I ask you some questions?"

"No, that's fine."

She motioned to Hannah to bring a chair over for him, and they both sat.

"When was the last time you saw Catherine?" Erica asked.

"When she left for work at seven-thirty this morning."

"Is that the normal time she leaves?"

He wiped his eyes and nodded. "Yes, every morning. She's like clockwork. She's one of those people who has a routine and sticks to it. She eats her breakfast at the same time each day—always a bowl of muesli with yogurt and a cup of tea—and puts on her makeup in exactly the same way at the same time. Nothing was different this morning."

"Did she mention that anything was worrying her?"

"She had some work stuff going on, but I didn't really understand it, to be honest. There's nothing unusual in that, though," he caught himself, "I mean the part about her having work stuff, not that I didn't understand it. She's in a high-paid job, and it's pretty much expected that there's going to be stress that comes along with that."

"Did she mention any names in particular?" Erica asked. "Anyone that we can follow up with?"

"No, sorry. You'd be better off asking at her office."

"Don't worry, we will be." Erica paused for a breath. "What about outside of work? Was she having any problems? Any money issues, or with drink or drugs, or gambling? Anything that might give us an idea why she's caught this person's attention?"

"No, she doesn't have time for anything like that. All she does is work and then come home late. We eat dinner, watch a bit of telly, and go to bed. Then we get up the next day and do it all over again."

Was she sensing a little resentment in his tone? "How do you feel about her working all the time?"

"Honestly, I think there's more to life than earning money to pay a mortgage for the next twenty-five years, so that when you're old you have a house to live in, and then you die. I've always been more someone who has to work to live, but she lives to work. She always promised that she'd chuck it all in once we had enough in savings, and we could travel the world, but instead the bills kept getting bigger, and that time has never come." He swept the ball of his hand across his eyes. "And now it might be too late."

"Don't give up," she told him. "Catherine is still very much alive, and she needs you to be strong for her."

"I'm just glad we never had children. I can't imagine what the poor other man's family is going through."

"Do you know of him at all? Did Catherine ever mention his name or that of his wife, Nancy?"

"No, but then she might have, and I wasn't listening. She's always complaining about me not listening to her. Maybe she's right. I wish I had now." A tear trickled down his cheek. "I should have listened. I should have told her I loved her more."

"I'm sure she knows," she reassured him.

He pressed his lips together and nodded.

She saw him out of the office with promises to stay in touch and then wound her way through the busy throng of phones ringing and computer keys clicking to head back to her desk.

"Erica?" Shawn's hand on her arm stopped her. "I need to speak to you."

"What's up?"

"Water's coming into Richard's room again. Someone might not drain it. We're running out of time."

Erica gritted her teeth. "I wish everyone would stop saying that to me."

"But it's true. I know you weren't keen on the idea, but have you reconsidered bringing in Jasmin Webb to try and crack the location the video feed is coming from?"

"We've got our best people working on it," she said.

"That may be true, but they're not getting anywhere. We need someone who knows how to slide under the radar, someone who doesn't necessarily do things by the book."

She arched her brow. "You mean someone who knows how to break the law?"

He shrugged. "If it saves the lives of Richard Morrisey and Catherine Taura, does it matter?"

"I'll pretend I didn't hear that."

He cocked his head. "Is that a yes, then?"

"Do you really think she can help?"

"She might not even want to get involved. She doesn't have a great history with the police, but there's no harm in asking."

"Okay," she relented. "Let's do whatever it takes."

Chapter Sixteen

L ike most of the city, Jasmin was glued to her computer screen, watching the horror of the poor kidnapped people unfold. When she'd woken this morning, there had been a new link included in the previous video comments and pinned to the top. The link led to a livestream of a woman who appeared to be trapped in a sauna.

< She looks like she's getting a bit hot under the collar. >
< That poor woman. Why isn't anyone helping her? >
< Who's responsible for this? Surely the police could be doing more? >

Jasmin read them through. Why hadn't the police been able to track down where the video feed was originating from? She assumed whoever was responsible was hiding their IP address, but that shouldn't be too difficult to unravel.

Her phone rang, and she checked the screen. She didn't recognise the number. Could it be someone calling her about that job? She still hadn't given an answer as to whether she was doing it, and they were probably getting impatient.

She hesitated for a moment and then answered. "Yeah?"

"Jasmin?"

The voice was male, and even from that single word, she was able to tell that it didn't contain any aggression. Did she even recognise it?

"Yeah," she repeated. "Who's this?"

"It's your cousin, Shawn Turner."

She had a flashback to several years earlier, when she'd still been a kid, going to a funeral of a distant relative and Shawn

125

being there. Some people in the family had turned their backs on him when he'd decided to join the police, but it didn't bother her at all. Sure, she'd had some issues with the cops herself when she'd been younger, but she'd freely admit that she'd brought that on herself. Besides, she was smarter now, more careful. Back then she'd been young and stupid.

"Oh, sure, Shawn. Hi. How are you?"

"I'm good. Sorry I haven't been in touch much. Been busy with work and stuff."

She still didn't have any idea why he was suddenly calling her. "That's okay," she said hesitantly.

"Listen, have you heard about what's been happening with two people being kidnapped and then streamed online?"

She perked up at the mention of them. "Everyone's heard about that. I've been watching the streaming."

"I'm working on the case."

"Seriously? Wow, shit. That's cool." She didn't understand why he was telling her.

"I guess so, but I'm not calling to brag or anything." There was a smile in his tone. "I actually wanted to ask for your help."

"My help? What can I do?"

"From what I remember, you can do a lot. I've never met anyone who knows their way around a computer better than you, and that was when you were a kid. I can't imagine what your skills are like now."

She hesitated and then said, "Maybe I gave up messing with computers after what happened."

Was this some kind of trap? Had he got wind of the job she'd been offered, and this was his way of catching her out before she got in too deep? She couldn't imagine he'd want to see her behind bars—and it wasn't like she'd actually done anything *yet*. Or maybe he was after the people offering her the job and wanted to use her?

"Did you?" he said. "I find that hard to believe."

"Why?"

"Because it's in your blood. It would be like a writer giving up writing, or an artist stopping painting. I can't see that happening."

"Maybe I grew up."

"I know you did, but I highly doubt you left it behind. I could always ask your mother?"

"No, don't do that," she said quickly, her gaze lifting to the ceiling, above which her mother sat in the living room. "You're right, I'm still—" she almost said 'working' and then caught herself. "Still involved in computers."

He gave a laugh. "That's an interesting way of putting it."

"You know what I mean."

"Look, we need some help over here at the office. As I'm sure you're aware, we might be running out of time to help the victims, and while we've got our best people trying to track down where the feed is coming from, I'm not sure it's going to be enough. We need someone who maybe knows different systems."

She arched an eyebrow, though he couldn't see her. "You mean ones that aren't necessarily legal."

"Well...yes."

She still wasn't sure. Was this going to get her in trouble? She pulled the screen up showing the man in the chair, and then flicked back to the woman in the sauna. The number of viewers and comments were increasing as every minute went by. She didn't want to watch anyone die online, assuming that was what was going to happen once the clock ticked down to zero.

"Do you have any idea who's behind this yet?"

"Not yet, but we're working on it."

"Whoever it is wants a big audience, that's for sure."

A pause came down the line, and then he said, "That's what we're afraid of."

Jas took a breath. "Okay, I want to help, if I can."

"Thanks, Jas. Are you still at your home address?"

"Sure am. Can't afford to move out."

"I hear you. I'll be over within the hour to pick you up and bring you in, and then we can debrief you in the office. You'll be expected to keep this to yourself."

"I understand."

She ended the call, sat back, and blew out a breath. Well, today had certainly taken a turn that she hadn't expected. What were people going to do and say if they found out she'd been working with the police? She doubted the other offer of a job would still be open if they got wind of it. They'd assume she was some kind of nark who couldn't be trusted.

Maybe it was for the best. She could have definitely done with the cash—it might have even been enough to finally afford a rental deposit—but these people's lives were more important.

Chapter Seventeen

The water had started to go down again.

Thank God.

Richard had believed he was going to drown. It was the most terrifying experience of his life—even more than during the birth of their son when Nancy had started bleeding and the doctors hadn't been able to stop it. For what must have been an hour, but what had felt like a lifetime, he'd pictured his future stretching ahead of him with a dead wife and a newborn. He had no idea how to take care of a baby by himself. But then the doctors had managed to stop the bleed and had given Nancy a blood transfusion, and she had been fine. Nancy had always been stronger than him. She'd acted as though nothing had happened, though he was sure she must have been frightened, too. She hadn't even got to say hello to her newborn baby properly before she'd been whisked off to theatre. She'd never even really mentioned it again.

The thought of his family brought fresh tears to his eyes. Did they know what had happened to him yet? He assumed whatever the camera was recording was being sent to someone—most likely his family to ask for a ransom or something. He hoped Nancy had done her best to protect the children from what was happening, though it wouldn't be easy. She was a good mother. Plenty would say that she worked too much, but then they would never have said that about him if their roles were reversed. Nancy was an excellent role model. Their kids would go on to aspire to do well in life because of her.

Whoever was doing this was deliberately trying to torture him. The water had risen and then drained away again several times now. It had reached his chin, making him strain to sit up straighter, to lift his backside from the chair to create more space. In his mind, he saw the murky water start to trickle over his face, fill his nose and mouth and eyes, until he eventually had no choice but to inhale it into his lungs.

But before it got to that point, the water stopped rising, and painfully slowly, over the space of hours, drained away again.

Who was the man who'd spoken when he'd first woken here? They'd said something about reaching a million viewers, but that couldn't be right.

No one had been in here to see him or bring him anything. He was weak with hunger, and, though he'd been surrounded by water, he hadn't been able to bring himself to drink any of it. For one, it wasn't clean, but also the thought of lowering his face into it would feel too much like he was drowning. He worried that he'd lose control and do something crazy like drown himself anyway.

At some point, though, depending on how long this went on for, he'd have no choice but to take a drink of the murky water. He could last without food, but not fluid.

A famous line about water being everywhere but there not being a drop to drink went through his head, and he suppressed a crazed laugh.

He was dripping wet, his clothes soaked to the skin. He shivered constantly.

At least he wouldn't need to piss himself so much. He worried about needing to take a shit, though.

That he'd been reduced to such a pitiful man so quickly whittled away at any remaining self-confidence.

"Please, if you can hear me, let me go. We have money, if that's what you want. A lot of money. If I die in here, you won't see a penny!"

He paused, his ears straining. Was anyone nearby? He hadn't heard footsteps. What even was this place? With the dank temperature, the damp, the concrete floors and stone walls, he felt like he was being kept in a kind of manmade cave, but he knew there was power or the lights and camera wouldn't be working.

He'd never known isolation like it. The sense that he was utterly alone. Even with the camera blinking at him, he still didn't get the sense that anyone was around.

He'd always considered himself a proud, strong, respectable person, but now he'd been reduced to a creature just trying to survive.

"Please," he said again, his voice small. A tear slipped down his cheek. "Please, someone...anyone...help me."

Chapter Eighteen

A man was waiting for Erica in the reception area.

"DI Swift," said the woman who worked as front counter staff, "this is Doctor Stock. He's here about Catherine Taura."

Erica noted to herself that Dr Stock was something of a silver fox. With his thick greying hair and intense blue eyes, he reminded her of that television chef people were always going on about.

She put out her hand, and he shook it.

"Thank you for giving us your time, Dr Stock," she said.

"Oh, please call me Rupert."

"In which case, I'm Erica. Come on through."

She led him into one of the interview rooms and gestured for him to sit down.

"I was hoping to get your professional opinion on Catherine Taura and her situation," she said.

"How many hours do you believe she's been in there now?" he asked.

"It's been more than we'd like."

"In which case, there's no possibility that the sauna is at the temperature of a regular sauna, which is normally about sixty-five to ninety degrees Celsius. She would most likely be dead already from dehydration and internal burns. Previous cases of women being trapped in a sauna have resulted in death within ninety minutes."

"Jesus. That's awful." She thought for a moment, biting at the skin on her lower lip. "It's good news for Catherine, though, right? If she's not dead yet, then she's not only got more time, but also the sort of stress her body would be under at those higher temperatures will be less than we were predicting?"

"That's right. When you enter a sauna, your heart rate goes up, your blood vessels dilate, and the blood flow increases to the skin. The sympathetic nervous system needs to become more active to maintain the temperature in the body. Assuming the sauna is heated, but not those temperatures, the biggest risk currently is dehydration. Catherine is most likely feeling sick and lightheaded, she's probably got a headache and is thirsty."

"We've watched her take a drink from the water that's supposed to be poured onto the hot coals to create steam."

"That's good." He nodded. "It means she hopefully won't be suffering any of the more life-threatening causes of dehydration."

"Which are?" she prompted.

He exhaled a long breath through his nose. "Kidney failure, seizures, hypovolemic shock, and eventually unconsciousness leading to a coma, and then most likely death. The good news is—if we can even call it good news—that Catherine is physically well. She takes care of herself. She's not over or underweight. According to her husband, she goes to exercise classes several times a week, she eats healthily, and she only drinks moderately and doesn't smoke. Those things will all go in her favour. She doesn't have any chronic illnesses that we're aware of, and no history of heart issues in her family. Of course, it's impossible to know for sure how her body will react to the amount of stress it's being put through right now, but she's at least in a good place physically to be able to cope with it."

"Assuming whoever is doing this doesn't turn up the temperature dial anytime soon?"

"Well, yes, and that's something we have no control over."

Watching these poor people suffering twisted Erica inside. She desperately wanted to save them, but right now, they still had no idea where they might be. The circle they'd created around Richard Morrisey's home was still an area that covered fifty square miles. It wasn't as though they could send teams of police searching every single home and building in the area.

"Can I ask you to stay nearby?" she said. "If there's a change in either of the victim's conditions, I'd like to know about it."

"Of course. I'll do whatever I can."

The water was on the rise again for poor Richard. Where the previous day, he'd struggled and tried to free himself, now he looked as though he'd already given up. He was slumped in the chair, his chin on his chest. Every so often, his eyes drifted shut, his head bobbed, and then he'd jerk himself awake again. He must be exhausted as well as being terrified.

Erica saw the doctor out and then went to update DCI Gibbs.

"I wish I had better news," she said, "but we're still nowhere near finding either the victims or the people responsible. I've got the press hounding us, and the story is blowing up on the internet. I feel like there must be a way we can use this to our advantage."

"What are you thinking?" he asked.

"Maybe using the exposure to try and get a message out to whoever is doing this? There must be something they want. No one threatens another person's life without reason."

"You think we should use the press to communicate with them?"

"It might be worth a shot. It'll give the press something to run with and let the kidnappers know we want to communicate. If we can find out what they want, maybe they'll release the victims."

He blew out a breath, sat back, and steepled his fingers in front of his lips. "We don't negotiate with terrorists."

"We don't know that these are terrorists. It could be pure coincidence that Richard Morrisey was chosen because he's the husband of a politician. We can't allow ourselves to be blindsided by that. Catherine isn't a politician. Would you consider what she's going through to be a terrorist threat?"

"We can't look at these cases individually. It has to be considered as a whole."

"Let us try to make contact with them," she pressed. "We've put comments beneath the live feed, but nothing is grabbing their attention. They might not even be reading them, for all we know. Maybe it's time we made a statement to the press, let them carry our words to the ears of those responsible."

"What are you going to say?"

"Plead to their sense of morality and hope they have one."

He gave a cold chuckle. "Do your best, Erica."

"Thanks, boss."

Half an hour later, Erica stood on the steps outside of the office. Cameras flashed, and reporters shouted over the top of each other. She lifted a hand to silence them all.

"As I'm sure you're all aware by now, the abductions of two people, Richard Morrisey and Catherine Taura, are being livestreamed on the internet. As of yet, we've received no communication from whoever is responsible for taking them. I want to address them now." She focused on the camera of the largest of the news stations. "Please, talk to us. Tell us what it is you want. Don't allow two innocent people to die for no reason. Richard is a father to two young children. Catherine is a beloved wife and daughter. They don't deserve what's happening to them. You can contact us through our crime line number. Help us to bring this to an end without anyone getting hurt."

Her voice died off, and those of the reporters rose once more, all shouting questions at her.

"I'll bring you another update when we have one," she said and turned from the crowd and went back inside the building.

Chapter Nineteen

Erica ordered food to be delivered for the team. She might have had the chance to grab a sandwich, but she knew how hard everyone was working, and plenty wouldn't have had the same opportunity. These little touches were always appreciated—and people who felt valued worked harder—but she was also aware that it meant keeping people in the office. With the number of reporters still hanging around, desperate to get a juicy headline for their newspapers, it was worth it to keep the team away from them.

"Erica," Shawn said, getting her attention. He wasn't alone. "I mean DI Swift, this is my cousin, Jasmin Webb. She's agreed to help us, and as you know, there's no time to waste, so I brought her straight here."

The young woman was beautiful. Big dark eyes, thick eyelashes, high cheekbones. Baggy sweatpants hung from her hips, and a tiny top exposed her belly. On her feet were white trainers, and heavy gold jewellery hung around her neck and wrists. She wore her beauty in the unaware way the young often did.

"I'm DI Erica Swift." Erica held out her hand. "Thank you for coming."

Jasmin glanced at Erica's hand and quickly shook it. "I don't even know if I can do anything to help yet."

"I appreciate you even trying. Honestly, I hate to admit it, but we're at a loss here. Nothing is bringing up any leads. I assume you've seen the feed online?"

Jasmin nodded. "Yeah, I've seen it. I did wonder if it had been staged—a publicity stunt for something, but it looks real to me."

"We believe it's real. We've tracked down the victims' families, and the victims are both missing."

"That must be so scary for them."

"Yes, it is," Erica agreed. "That's why we need to find them. The first man is called Richard Morrisey. He has a wife and two young children who desperately want him home. The second victim is called Catherine Taura, and she works for a large energy company, and she's married. But listen, Jasmin, I want you to know that if you're not able to find anything that might help us, it isn't your fault. This isn't your responsibility at all. Okay? A whole team of trained police haven't been able to find them, so please don't put it on your shoulders if this doesn't work."

It was the thing Erica was most worried about, especially now she'd seen just how young the girl was. What if these two people were killed, their deaths streamed on social media, and Jasmin mentally took responsibility for it? She didn't want the girl to feel that way, but what could she do? They had literally tried everything and come up empty-handed. Now they were desperate.

"It's okay, I understand. I want to help. I've been following the story, like most people have, and I can't believe someone would go to this level to make a point."

Erica eyed her. "You think whoever is behind this is making a point?"

Jas shrugged. "What else could it be?"

Erica gave the girl a nod and turned to Shawn. "Can you get her set up at a station and take her through the paperwork?"

"No problem." He jerked his head. "Come on, cuz."

Shawn led her away, and Erica went back to her desk. She wasn't alone for long. Karl approached, his expression pinched. Had he found something? She hoped he had news for her.

"Are you serious, Erica?" he said. "You brought in outside help?"

Erica let out a sigh. This was the last thing she needed. He clearly had his nose put out of joint, thinking Jasmin being here meant she thought he couldn't do his job.

"Look, I didn't like the idea either when Shawn suggested it—"

"So tell her to go home. We don't need some teenager interfering."

"She's good at what she does. Shawn vouches for her."

He curled his lip. "I should talk to Gibbs about this."

She raised her eyebrows. "Seriously, Karl? You want to go behind my back and do that?"

He shifted uncomfortably.

Erica continued. "I think he'd agree that finding these people and saving their lives is more important than worrying about your pride."

"Fine," he muttered and stormed back across the office.

Erica gave a groan and let her forehead drop to the desk. She only briefly debated banging her head against it several times.

Chapter Twenty

It was late by the time Erica got back home.

The remainder of the afternoon had proven to be fruitless. Jasmin hadn't managed to break through the VPN, and none of their leads had amounted to anything.

She probably should have told Shawn that she needed to get to bed, but she hadn't wanted to sit in an empty house all evening. He was swinging by his place to change, and then grabbing a curry on his way over.

The pull of her phone had turned into an addiction. She couldn't seem to stop herself watching the livestreams of the two victims, and at this rate she was going to spend all night staring at her phone, terrified that some new and terrible development would happen.

Erica was relieved when the doorbell rang and she had an excuse to put it down.

She opened the door to her partner and stepped back to allow him in. The savoury, spicy scent of the food he had clutched in one hand hit her nose, and her stomach gurgled. She hadn't realised how hungry she was.

"Beer?" she offered, letting him into the house. "I've got some zero percent ones if you're driving."

He shut the door behind him. "Sure. Unless you want me to stay here. Keep you company."

She didn't miss the flirty tone to his voice. The truth was, she didn't really want to be on her own.

"You could stay," she said. "There's a spare bed as Poppy's not here."

"Right. I'll take that drink then."

They went through into the kitchen, and Shawn dumped the bag in the middle of the kitchen table. Erica took a couple of chilled bottles of beer from the fridge while Shawn grabbed some plates. He didn't need to ask where anything was kept—he probably knew his way around the kitchen as well as she did.

Erica cracked open the beers and handed one to him. It would be the only drink either of them would be having. While they had people who'd taken over their shifts at work, Erica was still very conscious of the case in progress and the possibility they might be needed.

They clinked the necks of the bottles together.

"Cheers," Shawn said. "How does it feel not having Poppy in the house?"

"Weird. I keep feeling like I'm missing something, or I've lost something."

They took a seat at the table, and Shawn opened the lids of the plastic containers.

She'd gone for a chicken jalfrezi. He'd had the butter chicken. They had a pilau rice and a naan to share. They fell quiet for a moment as they dished up the food.

He leaned over to spear a piece of her food up with his fork.

"Hey, you've got your own," she protested.

"We can share, can't we? You have a bit of mine, I'll try some of yours."

"You want me to give up my real curry for your chicken in sauce?"

"It's good to have a bit of variety."

"Help yourself. I won't eat all this anyway. But don't come crying to me if it's too hot for you."

"Nah, I'm tougher than I look."

"You don't seem all that tough to me," she teased.

He squared his shoulders and raised his chin. "I can be tough." He planted his elbow on the table and gestured at her with his fingers. "Try me."

She arched her eyebrows. "You seriously want me to arm wrestle you?"

"Yeah. Try and beat me."

"I wouldn't want to embarrass you."

He wiggled his fingers. "Try it."

Unable to resist a challenge, she pushed her plate out of the way, half stood, and leaned across the table to grip his hand in hers. She held his eye. "You know this is going to—"

Before he'd had the chance to brace himself, she pushed his hand down to the table.

"Hey, that's cheating," he objected but didn't let go of her hand.

She didn't know how it happened, but one moment he was holding her hand in his, and the next he'd yanked her across the table, and they were kissing. Had she kissed him, or had he kissed her? Did it even matter?

She broke away. "Shit, Shawn. I'm sorry. I didn't mean for that to happen."

"Yes, you did, and so did I."

"We've been here before...We've already gone over all the reasons why this isn't going to work."

He shook his head in disappointment. "Come on, Erica. It's not like I'm some young, naïve new recruit who you've taken advantage of. Besides, most of the office think we're at it anyway."

She widened her eyes. "They do not!"

"Yes, they do, and it's not as though they're completely wrong, is it. There's been something between us for a long time now. They'd have to be blind to miss it."

"Do you think DCI Gibbs..." She trailed off.

"I think Gibbs cares about you and wants you to be happy, just like I do."

Her emotions warred inside her.

He got up and rounded the table and pulled her to her feet. "We'll keep things quiet, okay? No one else has to know our business. If things start getting too complicated, we can think again."

"Think again? About us?"

"About how this is going to work, because we *will* make it work, Erica. You know that. There's no one else but you, and there never will be."

Instinctively, to protect herself and perhaps wanting to protect him, too, she wanted to argue with him, to tell him there was no way he could know that. But she also respected him too much to dismiss his feelings in such a way. Besides, didn't she feel the same way? It had taken her a long time to get over losing her husband—she wasn't sure she ever would really—but in all that time, the only person who'd ever come close was Shawn.

There was no one else for her either, and she couldn't see there ever being.

"I'm frightened," she admitted.

"What of?"

"Of change. Of going through something so life-shattering again that I'm not even sure if the ground is still beneath my feet. I'm frightened for Poppy, too—"

He cut her off. "You know I'd never do anything to hurt Poppy."

"Yes, I do, but this is a dangerous job, and opening her up to that kind of loss again if something were to happen to you..."

He softened his tone. "She's already experienced that loss, Erica. She already has me in her life."

He was right. Of course he was. Was it even Poppy she was really worried about? Or was she actually talking about herself?

He touched his forehead to hers. "You know this is crazy, right? No job is worth giving this up for. We keep it to ourselves for now, and I'll move teams if it becomes a problem. I love you, and I love Poppy. I want to be here for you both."

Her heart ached. It felt like no matter what choice she made, she was going to lose.

Poppy loved Shawn, too. It had been years since Poppy's dad had died, and it broke Erica's heart that Poppy struggled to remember him now. But she was still young. Didn't she deserve to have a father figure in her life. And what better person could she ask for than Shawn?

"Tell me you don't want this?" He took her hand and placed it to his chest. "We're partners, in every sense of the word. We're meant to be, and you know it."

Her self-resolve crumbled. Maybe it would be okay. No one needed to know. She was sure her team already thought there was something going on between the two of them, and she guessed they had every reason to.

Her body softened, and his hand moved from hers to slip around her waist. He placed his palm against her cheek, his fingers in her hair. She looked up to him. Then his mouth was on hers, and her entire body seemed to be drawn to his, like two magnets locking together.

He kissed her, and she forgot everything else, all her worries and angst.

He took her hand and said, "Let's go upstairs."

She glanced at the table. "What about the food?"

"Erica, who gives a shit about the food? Let's go upstairs."

So they did.

Chapter Twenty-One

Jasmin took a sip of her energy drink and stared down at her phone as she walked from the bus stop to her flat.

She could have easily stayed in the office all night, but they'd insisted she go home and sleep. She didn't know how anyone was supposed to sleep when they had this hanging over them. Those poor people literally had a matter of hours until they were most likely killed, and she was supposed to forget that and go and lie down in bed?

No chance.

The weight of someone's gaze on her back had her glancing over her shoulder. It wasn't as though it was the middle of the night, so there were still plenty of people around, either making their way home or else heading out for the evening. Something sent the hairs on the backs of her arms rising, however, and she shuddered as though someone had walked across her grave.

She was most likely just spooked after watching those two people being traumatised on the internet. It wasn't surprising that she was anxious as well.

Jas quickly brought up Catherine Taura's livestream, checking she was still okay. It was hard to tell much through the foggy glass door, but she appeared to be sitting up, her bottom on the floor, her back pressed up against the lowest set of wooden benches. A doctor had been in and confirmed that Catherine was in good health, with no underlying conditions, so assuming the temperature was a survivable one for now, there was no reason to think her life was in imminent danger.

She switched to Richard Morrisey's feed. After reaching a high around five, the water had started to drain away again. Poor bastard. Someone was definitely messing with him.

Which would she prefer? To be trapped in that heat or chained to the chair in the water? She thought she'd choose the heat. At least Catherine got to move around a little. Neither option was exactly great, though.

Jasmin reached her front door, used her key in the lock, and entered.

"Hi," she called in a singsong voice. "I'm home."

Her mother stuck her head out from the kitchen. "Where have you been, Jas?"

Jas frowned. She was an adult and didn't usually need to report what she was doing back to her mother. Of course, she let her know when she was going to be late, purely out of courtesy, but it wasn't as though it was midnight.

"I told you. I've picked up a job. Why?"

"There were a couple of men here asking after you."

Jas paused. "What kind of men?"

"I don't know. White. In their late twenties, early thirties."

"Did they look like the cops?"

"No. If they were, I'm sure they'd have showed me some ID or something." She pursed her lips in a moue of disproval. "You're not in trouble with the police again, are you, love?"

Jas rolled her eyes. "No, Mum. I'm not in trouble with the police. I've been helping them with something."

"You have?"

"No need to sound so surprised. All the time I've spent sitting at the computer is worth something, you know."

"I know that." Gloria offered a smile. "You're a smart girl. I honestly don't know where you get it from. It's all like another language to me."

Who were the men who'd come asking after her? Did they have something to do with the investigation? No, they couldn't be connected because then they would have known she was at the office and not at home. Had someone found out that she was working on the case?

That made more sense. Word had probably got around, though she didn't know how since she'd been sworn to secrecy.

"Do you think they might have been reporters?" she asked.

Gloria considered this and then nodded. "Yes, that's most likely who they were, though they didn't leave a card or anything asking you to get in touch."

"Maybe they knew I'd tell them to get lost."

Her mother chuckled. "Yes, you would have."

Jasmin wondered if she should tell Detective Swift about this or maybe even Shawn. She still struggled to think of Shawn as being a detective. No one in their family saw the police as being a good thing, never mind actually becoming one of them.

She checked her phone for the time. It was getting late. The police probably had more important things to worry about than a couple of reporters hassling her. And it wasn't as though they'd caused trouble or anything. They'd rung her front doorbell and left again when she wasn't in. That was hardly a crime.

"Let me fix you something to eat," her mother said. "You need to eat."

There was no point in arguing with her. "Okay, thanks, Mum."

"I'll call you when it's ready, and then you can tell me all about what you've been doing today."

"I had to sign a nondisclosure agreement, Mum. There really isn't much I can tell you."

Gloria flapped a hand. "I'm sure you can think of something."

Jas rolled her eyes again—her mother clearly didn't understand what nondisclosure meant—and went down to her room.

She checked the online streams of the poor victims again. The constant checking was starting to feel obsessive, but she couldn't ignore the constant pull of her phone.

The magnitude of what she was trying to achieve hit her in the chest, stealing her breath. How was it possible that she held the lives of these people in her hands? What would happen if she failed? So many times, she'd been so close to cracking the code that was being used to switch the source of the video streams, but each time something had changed, throwing her off again.

How was she going to feel if these people died? Would she be carrying that guilt around with her for the rest of her life?

Chapter Twenty-Two

As had become her habit over the past couple of days, the moment Erica opened her eyes, she checked her phone. Though deep down she was sure one of her team would have already informed her if one of the victims had died overnight, she was still sick with worry.

Shawn was no longer in bed with her, and the rumble of the kettle boiling came from downstairs. She found herself smiling. It was such a small thing, but she couldn't remember the last time she hadn't needed to get up to make a coffee for herself. To have someone do that for her meant a lot.

Tearing her thoughts from the man downstairs, she quickly scrolled through to find out what had happened overnight.

The world seemed to vanish around her, and her vision tunnelled in on the small screen in her hand. A man lay on a metal-framed bed in a room. The mattress was bare beneath him. He only wore a pair of dirty pants, that appeared more grey than white, but that wasn't the most shocking thing about it.

The man resembled a famine victim. His ribs stood out in contrast to the hollows between them. His stomach was concave. His arms resembled sticks.

A wash of hot and then cold swept over her. Looking at him made her uncomfortable. She could make out the rise and fall of his hollow chest, so he was clearly still alive, though his eyelids were shut over sunken eyes.

Jesus Christ. What had happened to him?

With her phone still in her hand, she leapt out of bed, yanked on some clothes, and hurried downstairs.

"Have you seen this?" she blurted.

Shawn turned to her with a smile. "Good morning to you, too."

She didn't return the expression. "Sorry, but seriously, have you seen this?"

"What is it?" Shawn asked, his features drawing down to match hers.

"There's a third victim. A third stream has gone live."

Shawn held out his hand. "Let me see."

She trembled as she handed over the phone. Like with the other two, a countdown clock was in the corner of the screen. It was perilously close to the twenty-four-hour mark.

"Do we know when this went live?" Shawn asked.

She shook her head. "No idea, but there are already a ton of comments on it. It's gained traffic quicker than the other two because whoever is doing this has posted the link to the other videos, and obviously they've already built up a huge audience."

"What was the time when the first comment was posted?"

"Shit, of course."

Why hadn't she thought of that? She wasn't thinking straight. She was also out of sorts because she was dealing with this while also not having contact with her daughter. She understood it was supposed to increase the children's independence, but she didn't think it was reflective of the society they lived in these days. It was always possible to get in touch with someone.

"The first one was posted a little over an hour ago," she said.

"Is this someone who's gone missing recently then?" Shawn asked. "Like the others—snatched and then streamed online?"

"Maybe, but look at the state of him. He's not in a good shape at all."

"Cancer patient," Shawn suggested. "Or someone with an eating disorder."

"Possibly, but whatever has happened to him, I doubt he's got long left."

"This is insane. Who is this man?"

"We're going to need to get into work and do whatever we can to find out."

They were running out of time. By tomorrow morning, all three victims might be dead, and they were still no closer to finding them, and now there was another one.

She was failing them.

"Wait. We can't go in together. I'll go first, and you follow."

"Yes, boss." He gave her a wink. "I'll give it ten minutes. How about I pick up coffee first since we haven't had the chance to drink what I've made?"

"Sounds good. I think we're going to need it."

She hurried back upstairs to use the bathroom and make herself at least partway presentable for work. She swapped places with Shawn.

"There's a spare key in the junk drawer in the kitchen," she told him, "near the kettle. Help yourself and lock up when you've gone okay?"

"See you soon."

They exchanged a brief kiss, and she found herself trapping a smile between the press of her lips. Despite the seriousness of the situation, a little flutter of happiness existed inside her that hadn't been there before.

She drove into the office, battling the traffic and swearing at stupid drivers under her breath.

By the time she walked into the office, word had already spread. She was relieved to see most of her team, and the additional people they'd brought in to help already there. The moment Shawn arrived, she'd call another briefing and make sure everyone was on the same page.

First, she got on the phone to Tina at Counter Terrorism.

"Have you seen?" Erica asked.

"Yeah, I've seen. Do we know who he is yet?"

"No, but the team is working on it."

"The press appeal didn't help then? No one got in touch?"

Erica gave a cold laugh. "Oh, plenty of people got in touch, but none of them were viable."

"I did warn you that would happen."

"I didn't need warning. This isn't my first rodeo, and I'm fully aware of how many timewasters like to get involved with these things. But I thought it was worth the risk." Erica took a breath. "Any news on your end as far as trying to figure out where these videos are being streamed from?"

"Sorry, we're still working on it. I assume you don't have news either?"

"No. They're smart. They know exactly what they're doing."

"Let me know if you figure out who victim number three is."

"Will do." Erica ended the call.

She didn't know why Counter Terrorism had even got involved. While she appreciated everything they did to keep the country safe, they hadn't provided anything useful so far.

She spotted Shawn entering the office and took the moment to gather everyone in the briefing room.

"I'd hoped this day wouldn't come, but we have a third victim, and, according to the countdown clock, we have less than twenty-four hours now. Just like with the previous victims, we need to find out the identity of number three. We need to do a screengrab of the victim's face and blow it up to use as a reverse image search. Because of the clear physical changes the victim has gone through—assuming he hasn't always been the weight he is now—it might be harder to narrow down his identity."

"I jumped on it the moment I saw there was a third victim," Karl said. "You're right in that it's harder. The search I did pulled up several hundred possibilities."

Erica nodded. "Thanks for getting onto that. We need to go through each of the images, pick out any metadata we can about them, and then cross reference that with any information we might have on file. Karl, if you can also send the screengrab over to misper, together with a description, in case they get any reports of someone matching his description."

"Will do."

"How's everyone getting on with finding the locations of the other two victims?" she asked the rest of the team.

They all went through what they'd been working on, but no one had anything concrete to go on. Feeling helpless, she sent them back to work to try and figure out the identity of the third victim.

It wasn't long before they had something.

"Boss, I think we've got a hit," Jon called out over the office. "He's fifty-three-year-old Hector Townsend. He's from Surrey and went missing a little over a month ago. It was thought that he had suffered a breakdown and possibly committed suicide, or else just wanted to disappear."

It rang a bell with Erica. "I remember reading about that case."

They hadn't been involved as it wasn't on their territory, but his photograph and name had been circulated for people to be on the lookout for him. She hadn't even recognised him, though.

Quickly, she pulled the case up on her computer and went straight to the image of the victim that had been on the misper case file.

Their victim was nothing like the handsome, well-groomed fifty-three-year-old in the photograph. It was a struggle to believe it was the same man. She used her phone to bring up the live feed and held it up next to the picture of what he looked like before he went missing. Her gaze darted between them, trying to match them together. It took a moment, but the likeness was there in the eyes and the shape of the nose.

How had he been reduced to that in a month?

Now he was more like a little wizened old man, his cheeks sunken, his eyes hollow. Any body fat had wasted away and left his skin with a strangely baggy appearance that had folded into wrinkles—like a deflated balloon. It wasn't as though he'd been in any way overweight beforehand, but now he was like a skeleton.

"Jesus, Christ," she muttered. "What's happened to him? Do we know if he had any kind of medical diagnosis? I'm not sure if even an aggressive form of cancer could do that to a person."

"He reminds me of a famine victim," Jon commented. "Like he's starving to death."

Erica paused, the comment sparking something in her brain. "What if that's exactly what's happening to him?" she half wondered out loud.

His eyes narrowed. "What do you mean?"

"We've got Richard Morrisey drowning. Catherine is being heated to death. And now he's starving? Someone is clearly trying to make a point."

Daniel Southern had suggested to her right at the start that this might be political, that Nancy Morrisey had dealt with protesters in the past. She hadn't given enough thought to exactly how that might work, but now she was thinking that he'd been right.

She remembered the security footage of the floodwater. Was that a hint at what was motivating them?

"What's the connection between the victims?" she asked.

"They're all white," Jon said, "and from a place of privilege and power. They're all wealthy."

She considered this. "You think this might be some anti-capitalist thing?"

Jon angled his head. "Possibly."

Erica took a breath and addressed the rest of the team. "You know the routine, folks. Let's find out everything we can about Hector Townsend."

This one should be easier since they already had a misper case open about him. Erica checked up the name of the SIO on the case, DS Raphe Contrell of the Surrey Police force. She found his number and gave him a call.

"I believe we've located one of your misper victims," she started and then had to correct herself. "At least, not located, as such, but we might have a lead on Hector Townsend. He went missing a month ago."

"That's right," DS Contrell said. "What have you got?"

"Have you been aware of the videos that have been playing online over the past few days? The ones that appear live with the countdown clock in the corner?"

His tone grew firm. "Of course. I think the whole country has been glued to those livestreams. Is that your case?"

"Yes, it is."

"And you think it's connected to my case?"

"Have you seen there's a third victim?" she asked. "They only appeared this morning."

"No, I've been busy with something else. You think one of the victims is Hector Townsend? The millionaire?" He blew out a low whistle. "Are you sure?"

"Give me your email, and I'll send the two images for comparison."

He gave it to her, and she clamped the phone between her ear and her shoulder as she typed out the message and added the images and a direct link to the site.

"Obviously," she continued, "we haven't been able to do any DNA or print checks to confirm his identity, we're going on the images alone, but it certainly appears to be the same man." She corrected herself. "At least, it does if you take into account his appearance now. Can you open the files and the link I just sent you?"

"Yes, I—" he started and then cut himself off. "Jesus Christ. What happened to him?"

"Unless we learn otherwise, there's a chance whoever took him has been deliberately starving him. It's early in the investigation yet, but it matches up with the kind of torture the other victims are being subjected to—one is almost drowning, the other is being heated to within an inch of her life."

"What sick bastards are responsible for this?"

"That's what we're trying to find out. We could use your help, to bring us up to speed on Hector Townsend's case, let us know if you ever had any leads, that kind of thing. As you can see by the clock, we're running out of time."

"You think whoever's doing this will kill them when it hits zero?"

"It's a serious possibility."

"But no one has come forward to claim this yet?"

"No, which is strange. We believe this to be politically motivated, but no one group has stepped forward yet."

"Okay, let me bring up Hector Townsend's file, and then I can bring you up to speed." There was a pause while DS Contrell did what was needed. "So, Hector Townsend is a millionaire, with numerous investments and businesses. He was last seen leaving his house a month ago. He was on foot. We had final proof of life via a Ring doorbell camera of his neighbour's property, but then he simply vanishes."

Erica sat back. "And that was it? No traces?"

"No, nothing."

"Was it ever considered that something bad had happened to him?"

"Yes, of course, but we had no proof of foul play. We never found any evidence of him receiving threats, and no one made contact to try and get money for his safe return. He was a grown man, and he was free to disappear, if he wanted."

"I see."

"He doesn't have any family," the misper detective continued, "and no real friends that we could find. Anyone we spoke to gave a picture of an extremely reserved, intense individual, who had very little in the way of social connections. His entire life seemed to revolve around his work, so when things weren't going well, we figured he must have taken it harder than most. If a person doesn't have any kind of support network, then these things can become overwhelming."

Erica picked up on something. "You said things weren't going well at his work?"

"That's right. He'd recently lost a lot of money. One of the companies he had a lot of shares in plummeted in value over the past twelve months."

"Let me take a guess in the company," Erica said. "Offshore Solutions Limited, by any chance?"

"Yes, how did you know?"

"It's the same company the female victim works for, and also one that's been lobbying Richard Morrisey's wife, Nancy Morrisey, and failed."

"That's the connection between each of the victims?" he asked.

"Right now, I believe so, yes. Maybe someone has a vendetta against the company?"

"A recently fired employee or something like that?"

It was something they hadn't actually looked into. "That's a good suggestion, thanks. We'll follow that up. But back to Hector Townsend... You thought he might have done something to harm himself?"

"It was definitely a consideration, yes. When we spoke to people he worked with, they'd all agreed that he'd been acting even more strangely than normal recently. They described him as having outbursts of anger and vanishing for periods of time, with them being unable to contact him. It was assumed he was depressed, so when he went missing, it was thought that he might have harmed himself."

"What about his phone or bank records?"

"The mobile phone was found at his house. The last call he made was a business one, and there was nothing we found to be suspicious about it. There were no records of him having received any threatening messages or calls either. We found no uses of his bankcards after the day he went missing."

"That didn't trouble you?"

"Yes, of course it did, but a man of his wealth could easily have stashed enough cash away somewhere for him to live on. He didn't necessarily need to have been using bank cards. He'd already created a pattern of being uncontactable for periods of time, so that he'd left his phone didn't surprise us either."

"What about his car?"

"It was left in his driveway, but again, with the kind of money he had, he could have easily had a second vehicle, and perhaps have it registered under one of his company names. We did check into any that might be missing, and didn't find anything, but he might have easily gone under the radar."

"Except he didn't," Erica pointed out. "He'd been snatched by whoever is behind holding these three people captive."

"Hindsight is twenty-twenty. We had no reason to believe anything bad had happened to him—at least nothing bad that he wasn't directly responsible for himself."

"Am I able to see the complete case file?" Erica asked. "I don't know if there will be anything that'll help, but you never know."

"Of course, and if there's anything else I can do to help, please let me know. I do feel responsible for not having found Mr Townsend sooner. No one wants a case to end like this."

"It's not over yet," Erica said. "We still have time."

Chapter Twenty-Three

"It would seem we have a connection between the victims," Erica told her team. "Hector Townsend has shares in the same company that Catherine Taura works for. Those shares have seen a massive decline over the past twelve months, meaning Hector has lost millions of pounds."

"Why has the company lost so much money?" Shawn asked.

Erica checked the notes. "It was rejected for a long-planned application to drill for oil in the North Sea."

"Why was it rejected?" he asked.

"A push for more green energy. The government are planning for a wind farm to be built there instead." A lightbulb flickered to life in her head. "And there's a chance that decision might have been partly down to Nancy Morrisey?"

"I guess so, yes. We'll need to speak to her directly about that."

Erica screwed up her face. "But if it is protesters behind this, why pick on Nancy Morrisey, or at least her husband? What did the kidnapper hope to achieve by doing this?"

"Making a point that people shouldn't be earning money by destroying the environment."

It still didn't make sense. "But Nancy Morrisey did the opposite of that. It was down to her that the windfarm was pushed through."

"True, but how many oil companies has she given the green light to in the past? Perhaps that one nod to cleaner energy wasn't enough. Maybe the climate change groups viewed it as virtue signalling?"

She blew out a breath. "Well, they're not doing themselves any favours by torturing innocent people."

"I guess they don't see them as being innocent, and according to the comments, plenty of others agree with them."

"Jesus Christ." She shook her head in dismay. "I think it's time we spoke to these climate groups, see if we can get any of them to own up to what's happening."

"You think that's likely?"

"No, but it's a start. Can you speak to Daniel Southern as well, find out if any of the groups in particular have been causing problems for Nancy."

Shawn nodded. "No problem. I'll give him a call. He did seem to think there was a particular group when this all first happened. Maybe we should have paid more attention to that?"

Erica tried not to kick herself. "Yeah, you're right. Dammit."

"We don't know for sure yet that we're on the right track."

Maybe not, but it was all starting to slot into place—the footage of the flood, the rising water, the overheating in the sauna, the starving of a wealthy man.

If this was a new way to protest, it had certainly got the world's attention.

Chapter Twenty-Four

J asmin sat at the desk she'd been given, reading through all the comments. There were hundreds of them. Plenty were clearly spam—trying to get people to click on dodgy links or offering work from home jobs that apparently paid a grand a day. What kind of idiots fell for that stuff?

There was a pattern in the comments, however—a theme to them.

Was it something important?

She got up to approach the desk of DI Swift. Jas would never have admitted it out loud, but she found the detective intimidating. She hoped she wasn't about to say something stupid.

"Can I speak to you for a minute?" Jas said.

DI Swift glanced up from her desk. "Yes, of course. What's up?"

"I've noticed something, and I don't know if it's important, but I thought I'd mention it."

A part of her worried she was going to get laughed out of here. She felt overwhelmed by a sense of imposter syndrome. These were actual detectives, older than her, too, while she was only a teenager who happened to have a knack for computers. But they'd brought her in for a reason, and if she didn't say what was on her mind, what was the point in her being here?

"I've noticed a pattern in the comments. Now, it might be that these accounts are bots or sock puppets—"

Erica lifted a hand to stop her. "I'm sorry—what puppets?"

"Sock puppets? They're fake accounts that are used to promote a certain agenda."

"I see. Carry on."

"So they might be fake accounts, in fact, they most probably are, but they all seem to be pushing the same thing."

Jas pulled up the comments on Richard's livestream.

<Thousands of people all over the world are drowning due to climate change. Why does no one give a shit about them?>

"And another one," Jas said.

<One third of Pakistan was underwater last year, and 1,400 people died, but no one cares about that. You only care about wealthy white people.>

"And check out this one."

<Billions of people in South East Asia are affected by flooding due to climate change. Maybe all you bleeding hearts should think about them instead?>

"They pop up about every ten comments, all of them commenting on flooding and climate change, and how it's affecting people. If you read Catherine's comments, it's the same, only it's talking about how the increase in the world's temperature is affecting our planet, melting ice caps and killing off the coral reefs."

"It does seem like they have an agenda," Erica agreed. "It fits with what we've been considering."

Jas rushed on, encouraged. "People are replying to the comments, too. Some agreeing, others telling them to get off their high horses, some dismissing climate change as another hoax. Whatever they're saying, they're getting people talking."

"Do you think this might be what they wanted all along? That there's a climate change group behind this?"

Jas shrugged. "Honestly, I don't know. It might be that they're seeing it as a platform to use to spread the word, but you have to admit that what the victims are going through does correspond to what the comments are saying."

DI Swift nodded slowly. "You're right, they absolutely do. Are you able to track down any of the identities of those leaving comments?"

"So, I already tried, and I believe each of them are using the same kind of VPN that is being used to run the livestream."

The detective's eyebrows rose. "What? All of them?"

"All the ones I've tried so far, but obviously I haven't been able to check them all. There are hundreds, and I doubt all of them will be. Even if those behind the kidnapping have written some of the comments, regular viewers will have jumped on the bandwagon and joined in, which is obviously something they're trying to encourage people to do."

Erica tapped her fingers on the desk while she thought. "If there was more time, I'd say we could use the comments themselves. A personal writing style is like a fingerprint. People don't realise they do it, but they use grammar and punctuation in their own individual way, or always misspell the same words. It can be used to identify someone if we've got something to compare it to. Unfortunately, we don't have that, and we don't have time to find something either."

"I could create a malware that would compromise the commenter's machine, but it would need one of the commenters to click on a link, and I suspect they're too smart for that."

"But they might do it," DI Swift said.

Jas wrinkled her nose and nodded. "They might, but in an open forum like that, so might a whole heap of other people. We can't narrow it down so it only infects the machines of whoever is behind this."

"Damn. What about the email addresses associated with the commenters' profiles?"

"Again, I'm happy to do some digging, but they're not stupid. If I'm right about them being the same person, they'll have protected themselves."

"If there's a climate change group behind this and they want to be heard," Erica said, "why aren't they stepping up and admitting to being the ones doing this?"

"Maybe they don't want to look like the bad guys?" Jas suggested. "They're getting people talking, pushing their agenda, without ever having to say that they're doing something terrible to innocent people to make it happen."

The detective offered her a smile. "Thanks, Jasmin. You've been incredibly helpful. I should have thought of that myself. Someone close to Nancy Morrisey already thought that this was politically motivated. It appears they were right."

Chapter Twenty-Five

"According to Daniel Southern," Shawn said, "there's one climate group Nancy has had issues with over the past couple of months. You've probably heard of them—The Climate Uprising?"

Erica had heard of them. "They're the ones who like to glue themselves to pavements and climb buildings. They seem to like disrupting people more than fighting for the environment."

"I guess they'd argue that it's impossible to get anyone to listen without making a nuisance of yourself. The whole point of a protest is that you get people to pay attention to you. That's not going to happen if you quietly hold up a sign and hope people will notice you."

"Is that what they're doing now? Trying to get people to listen?" She found herself bristling, defensive. If there was any chance that this group was behind the abductions, she didn't want Shawn defending them in any way.

He didn't seem to pick up on her mood. "Climate change is going to affect everyone, and people can keep ignoring it and letting big businesses focus only on making money, but when we're all either underwater or on fire, then they'll realise those protesters were right. By the time that happens, it'll be too late."

"They still can't abduct and torture people to send out a message."

He held up both hands in surrender. "Hey, that wasn't what I was saying." He thought for a moment. "What if they are just trying to make a point? What if the timer runs out and these people are set free."

"Can we really take that risk?"

"Probably not, but it's counting down, maybe in the same way they see the time we have left on the planet as counting down, unless something changes."

She shook her head. "This is insane."

"I guess they'd argue that doing nothing is the insane thing."

She didn't have time to argue with him. "Who's running The Climate Uprising? Do they have someone at their head, like a business would?"

It wasn't something Erica knew much about, she realised. All she knew of them was what she saw in the news or on social media where they seemed to be creating havoc with more and more elaborate protests. They glued themselves to roads, and climbed buildings and bridges, and defaced expensive art. Erica believed in the right to protest, but there were some things she didn't understand, especially defacing art. This, however, was on a whole other scale. They were implying these people would be killed when the timer ran out.

Shawn checked his phone for the information. "There are three people who cofounded The Climate Uprising back in twenty-ten. Their names are Colette Diamond, George Tither, and Waylen Dutton. George passed away a couple of years ago with cancer. And Waylen left the organisation about twelve months ago. Apparently, it wasn't going in the direction he'd hoped."

"Yeah, like resorting to kidnapping and imprisoning innocent people, and then streaming the footage online," she said. "So Colette Diamond is running the show now?"

"Certainly looks that way on paper."

"In which case, let's bring in Colette Diamond. See what she has to say for herself."

. . . .

THE WOMAN SITTING IN the interview room was nothing like Erica had been expecting.

Erica checked her own prejudices. Just because someone cared about the environment and the next generations' future didn't automatically mean they were a dread-locked, vegan hippy—not that there was anything wrong with being any of those things. But the woman sitting behind the table could have easily been sitting in a boardroom or even behind one of the desks here at the station.

Colette Diamond was in her forties, her dark hair knotted on top of her head, a pair of black-framed glasses on her straight nose. Her eyebrows were thick and full and expressive. No one would have thought this woman as being pretty, but she was certainly striking. Erica could see why people would follow her.

One thing she didn't look like was someone who would abduct three innocent people and stream the countdown to their possible deaths online, but appearances could be deceptive.

Erica had run a background check on Colette. She'd had a few minor charges against her—obstructing a police officer, public nuisance, obstructing a highway—essentially all the things Erica would have expected to see from someone who led a group known for their protests.

Erica had already run Colette through all the groundwork that came with being in an interview room. She wasn't under arrest—they didn't have anywhere near enough evidence to allow that—but she said she was happy to talk.

"The last thing I want to see is any harm coming to those poor people," Colette said. "I've been watching this unfold with the same amount of horror as anyone else. I want to do whatever I can to help."

Erica turned her laptop around to face the other woman. Onscreen was the footage of Hector Townsend. "Have you been reading the comments section? Every few comments, one pops up about climate change."

She winced. "I mean, I'm not going to pretend like it's a bad thing that people are talking about this. It's a big issue, and people should be talking about it. I *want* people to talk about it. But not like this."

Erica got straight to the point. "Where were you on Monday morning, between the hours of seven a.m. and ten a.m.?"

Colette folded her hands on the table. "I was with my husband and two teenaged children. I'm basically a glorified taxi for the kids now. They can all confirm my whereabouts." She took a resigned breath. "I understand why you're trying to pin this on us, but we're not the ones responsible."

"Is it possible someone is working without your knowledge?"

Colette considered this. "I'd like to be able to say no, but it's certainly possible for people to do things without me knowing about it. Do I think someone could pull off *this* kind of stunt, however? No, I don't believe any of our members would do something so terrible. We want to save lives,

Detective, not destroy them. This goes against everything we stand for and believe in."

"You're trying to tell me that you don't have members of your group who believe you should be doing more?"

"Of course, there are always people who go against the grain, but do I think any of them are capable of this? Absolutely not. We want the public to see us as the good guys, the ones who are fighting for their futures."

"Tell that to the people whose lives get disrupted by your protests," Erica said.

"People's lives are going to be more than disrupted for a few hours if our climate trajectory stays the way it is and no one does anything about it. It's impossible to protest without having some kind of impact on people's day-to-day lives. If we didn't, what would be the point? At least we get people talking, we get them thinking. But we don't want to ostracise the general public. We want them on our side. We want them to join us so there are more voices for the politicians and the big businesses to listen to. Doing something like this goes against all of that."

"But it's working, isn't it?" Erica said. "You said yourself that you want to get people talking...well, people are certainly talking now. No one's talking about anything else."

Colette let out a breath, took off her glasses, rubbed at the bridge of her nose, and then placed them back on again. "Our mission statement has always been non-violent protests. Sure, sometimes things get out of hand, but planning something that is clearly harming other humans is not what we're about."

The woman was impressing Erica. She spoke clearly and, while not lacking in emotion, she didn't let it overrule her either. She was direct and confident, and the fact she had a solid alibi for when Richard was taken meant she wasn't involved with the actual kidnapping of the victims. That didn't mean there weren't people in her organisation who had gone behind her back.

Erica hit play on the original video—the one where a voice had told Richard Morrisey that he had an audience. The words rang out in the room.

"What about this voice?" she asked. "Do you recognise it?"

Colette listened. "No, sorry. It's not familiar."

"Do you have anyone in your organisation who is especially good with computer technology? Someone who could setup a VPN that's impossible to trace?"

"Not that I know of. We have people who can work social media and set up a website, but that's about it."

"I'm going to need names of any troublemakers you've come across in your organisation, or anyone whose been pushing for your protests to have more of an impact. There must be someone."

By the purse of her lips and the flick of her eyes, Erica could tell the head of The Climate Uprising had thought of someone.

Erica took out her notepad and pen and pushed it across the table. "Write the names down," she said, nodding at the notepad, "together with any contact details you might have for them."

"Can I use my phone?" Colette asked.

"Of course. Like I said before, you're not under arrest for anything. You're simply helping us with our enquiries, and from what you've said, that's something you want to do."

Colette Diamond picked up the pen.

Chapter Twenty-Six

E rica took the list Colette had given her back to her team.
"We have several primary persons of interest," she told
them. "Their names are Ruby Walker, Tommy Biel, Elsie Smith,
and Gordie Carol. It's possible they've gone rogue, and though
they might believe they're fighting for our futures, they're
clearly going about it in the wrong way. I will not have
kidnappers go unpunished, no matter what their reasons
behind it."

"Do we know for sure they're the ones responsible?" Shawn
asked.

"Not yet, but we definitely need to talk to them. Let's do
our best to track them down."

Erica pulled up the live feed of the victims. At first, she
couldn't see Catherine Taura, but then she spotted her lying on
the floor.

That was worrying.

"Is she unconscious?" she wondered.

"It might be that it's cooler down there," Shawn pointed
out. "Heat rises, so it would make sense that the floor is at a
lower temperature."

Erica pressed lips together. "She's a smart woman. She'd
think of something like that."

She studied the screen for any sign of movement. Maybe
Catherine *was* only lying down, but then again, perhaps she
had some kind of undiagnosed heart condition and the
extended exposure to the high temperatures had caused her to
collapse.

The clock in the corner of the screen continued to count down. If whoever was behind this had intended for Catherine to die when the clock hit zero—perhaps by increasing the temperature in the sauna to a level that was impossible to survive—what would he or she do if Catherine's body gave out before then? Would it have spoiled their plans? Ruined the impact of the countdown? Would they find another victim to replace her?

Then Catherine lifted her hand and swept her damp hair away from her face, and Erica let out a sigh of relief. She was still very much alive, though she had no idea if she'd stay that way.

· · · ·

THE DAY WAS FAST DISAPPEARING.

"Tell Jasmin she can go home," Erica told Shawn. "I think she's done everything she can. She doesn't need to be here all night."

"I assume the rest of us will be?"

"Only if you want to be."

He offered her a hint of a smile. "I'm not going anywhere."

Half the team were out trying to track down the people Colette had named, but she addressed the rest of them. "We're onto our final twelve hours now. If you absolutely have to go home, then you can, but if you're willing to stay, then we'll appreciate your help."

"I can stay," Jas said. "I don't need to go anywhere."

Erica shook her head. "You're a civilian. We have others working on this. You should get some rest."

The girl seemed reluctant, but she stood and gathered her things. "I'm sorry I haven't been of more help."

"You've done everything you can."

"I hope you get a breakthrough overnight."

"Me, too." *Because any longer and it'll be too late.*

Jasmin left the office, and Erica sighed and raked her hands through her hair. She went back to the comments on the live feeds, searching for anything that might be a message from the people behind this.

Her phone rang. It was DC Hannah Rudd. "I just got word that we've picked up the two women Colette Diamond named."

"That's good news. Let's hope they know something."

"We could certainly use a break," Hannah said.

Erica would let her team interview the two women. They were perfectly capable, and it wasn't really her job anyway.

She called a briefing to ensure everyone who remained in the office was up to speed with the investigation, and to share anything they'd learned. They were making progress, but it all still felt frustratingly slow.

"Shit, have you seen this?" Shawn called over to her.

"What is it?"

"One of the local newspapers has got hold of the fact we're using a civilian on the case and that she has a juvenile conviction for hacking. They're calling us desperate."

"Dammit. Do they mention Jasmin by name?"

"Yes, they do. They've even got a picture of her."

"Someone has leaked her name," she said, furious. "Who the fuck did this?"

Shawn pressed his lips together. "It must be someone on our team. No one else knows."

She shook her head. "We don't know that for sure. Who has Jasmin told?"

Shawn stuck up for his cousin. "She knew to keep this to herself."

"She's still only nineteen. You remember how it felt to be that age? How you craved attention and approval from everyone. There was nothing more important than your peers. Maybe she was showing off to someone or trying to prove herself?"

"I'll give her a heads-up." Shawn put his phone to his ear. "She should know."

They both waited as the phone rang, but Shawn shook his head and ended the call again. "No answer. She might have the phone on silent or something."

Damn. Erica tried to tell herself it didn't mean anything, and Jasmin could be asleep or have gone out and forgotten her phone—not that many teenagers went anywhere without their phones these days—but that didn't stop her worrying. She wouldn't forgive herself if something happened to the girl.

"Keep trying," she told him.

Chapter Twenty-Seven

Jasmin tried not to feel the sting of rejection she'd experienced at being sent home while everyone else was being put to use.

She understood she wasn't one of the police, but she'd still wanted to help. That she hadn't been more help made her feel like a failure.

Back home, Jas made herself a bowl of ramen noodles, and she ate while barely tasting them, despite them being one of the spicier brands. Her computer here at home was nowhere near powerful enough to do what was needed. She was exhausted, but how could she sleep?

People's lives were literally in her hands.

Shortly before ten, Jas took a quick shower, brushed her teeth, and changed into a clean outfit.

Still indecisive, she hung around, debating what to do.

She should go back to the office, no matter what they'd said. She'd change her clothes and wash her face and then head back in there. It wasn't as though the place would close overnight. People would still be there, and she wasn't going to get any sleep anyway. When that counter hit zero, and she knew there was nothing more she could do, then she would get some rest.

Should she tell her mother where she was going? She didn't want to wake her. Instead, she left a note, explaining that she'd needed to go back into work. She'd have her phone with her, so her mum could still call if she needed to. It wasn't as though Jasmin was a child anymore, but she knew her mother still worried. The two of them were close. She should probably think about moving out sometime, but she didn't want to leave her mum all alone.

She padded up the stairs as quietly as possible and paused at the top. She strained her ears, trying to detect any sign of movement coming from her mother's bedroom. Only soft snores met her ears. She was definitely asleep.

Jas went to the fridge and grabbed another can of energy drink. She really needed to quit these things, they couldn't be good for her, but now wasn't the time. If it helped her stay awake and remain focused, then she'd drink however many she needed.

She'd take the bus and would walk the rest of the way.

Maybe some women would be nervous about travelling alone at this time of night, but Jasmin wasn't worried. This was her home, and she felt comfortable here, even if there was a psychopath around who was kidnapping people and broadcasting the possible lead-ups to their murders online.

The bus stop was on the high street, a couple of streets from home. She slipped out of her front door and closed it behind her, careful not to let it slam. It might be dark, but the city was far from being quiet. In the distance was the rise and fall of a police or ambulance siren. Someone chattered nearby. A television was on too loudly, the noise filtering out onto the street. She didn't feel like she was alone.

The tap-tap of footsteps came from somewhere behind her. She didn't want to look around. It would only make her both seem and feel more vulnerable if she glanced over her shoulder to see who was there. Should she take out her phone, maybe call someone? But then if this person wanted to rob her, she'd make it easy for them to steal it from her.

She picked up her pace, hoping to leave the owner of the footsteps behind, but as she walked faster, so did the person.

This wasn't good.

It suddenly seemed very dark and very late.

A figure stepped out of the road ahead of her, directly into her path.

"Excuse me," she said, keeping her head bent, one arm crossed in front of her body as she hung on to the strap of her bag at her shoulder.

The man snorted laughter. "I don't think so, bitch."

Her heart tripped, and she suddenly realised the person with the footsteps was now right up behind her.

She darted to one side, but they sandwiched her in, not letting her go anywhere.

"What is it you're doing for the police?" one demanded.

"What? Nothing." Shit, how did they know?

"Don't fucking lie to us."

She glanced around, desperate for someone to interrupt and offer her help. Why did they have a problem with her? Were they connected to whoever had taken those poor people? If so, she should try to get a good look at them, to be able to give their description to Shawn or his boss. That was assuming they let her walk away from this. Then again, they might just as easily be a couple of arseholes who'd read her name on the internet and decided they wanted to have some fun.

She knew there was no point in trying to argue with them or plead her case. These men had been waiting for her and most likely already knew exactly what they wanted to do with her. Nothing she said was going to make any difference. She had two choices: keep quiet and let them get whatever they planned over with...or fight like hell and run.

"What's the matter?" one teased in a singsong voice. "Cat got your tongue? You need to let those people die. They deserve it. Rich fuckers and politicians." He turned his head and spat on the ground.

With his focus off her, if only for a second, she took advantage of it. She darted to one side to get past him, but strong arms wrapped around her waist and hoisted her off her feet.

"Where do you think you're going?" the man said from behind her, his breath hot and stinking of stale cigarettes.

Both feet were off the ground and facing the man in front. She used the momentum, lifting her knees and kicking out at him like a kangaroo in a fight. By sheer luck, she caught him right in the stomach, and he folded in half. He gasped for breath, and she realised she must have winded him.

"Fucking bitch," the other one spat.

"Get off me!"

She kicked out and struggled, but he held her fast. If she didn't manage to get away before the other man regained his breath, things were going to get worse, fast. He had her arms pinned to her sides, and no matter how much she tried to get her feet to connect with his shins, she couldn't quite manage it. She remembered one part of her he didn't have control of.

Jas swung her head back as hard as she could. The back of her skull connected with the lower half of his face, and something cracked. Instantly, the tight band of his arms around her body released.

She didn't waste another second. The moment she was free, she ran.

His voice, thick with blood, chased her down the road.

"You fucking bitch. I should have you arrested for assault!"

Sometimes she wondered if people had any self-awareness at all. Didn't it even occur to him that they were the ones who'd assaulted her first? What she'd done had been out of necessity, it was self-defence, and yet they still framed themselves as being the victim.

No longer wanting to risk getting on the night bus, she kept a close eye over her shoulder, and finally, the yellow lights of a cab appeared down the road. She could have called an Uber, but she wanted to keep moving, worried those two pricks would lie in wait for her again.

She was worried it wouldn't stop for her—a young black woman on her own—but thankfully, the indicator light came on, and the driver pulled up beside her.

"Thank you," she said and went to the rear door. She opened it and climbed into the back seat.

"Where to?" he asked.

She gave him the address of the office.

In the rearview mirror, the driver frowned at her in concern. "You all right, love?"

She shook her head. "Yeah, I'm fine. Just drive, please."

Her heart raced, and she trembled all over. That experience could have had a very different ending. It had definitely shaken her. But the familiar interior of the black cab helped to calm her.

She took out her phone and swiped the screen to bring it to life. Her stomach dropped. There were multiple missed calls from Shawn. Shit. That would teach her to keep her phone on silent. Her hands trembled, and it took her a couple of goes to bring up the correct number, but eventually, she pulled up her cousin's. She hit the call button and placed the phone to her ear.

After a couple of rings, he answered. "Jasmin? Is everything all right?"

She discovered tears were suddenly close, tightening her throat painfully and pricking her eyes.

"Shawn. I was just attacked. It was two men."

"What? Are you all right?"

"Yeah, I'm okay. I'm in a taxi now. I'm coming in." She hesitated and then said, "It was like they were warning me off working on the case. I didn't know if they'd been put there to try to frighten me off, like they're worried I might be getting close to cracking it."

"Jesus. Can you give a description of them? Where did this happen? I'll send a response car, see if we can pick them up."

She gave him the location, and the best description she could manage, though she realised now how difficult it was to describe someone beyond sex, skin colour, and approximate age, especially when it was dark and they'd had hoods to cover their hair and partially obscure their faces. She'd also been in shock and trying not to panic.

"I'm sorry I can't be of more use."

"That is useful. We might be able to get some security footage from around that area, too, potentially catch them on camera."

She started to relax. "Thanks, Shawn." She thought of something. "Why were you trying to contact me? I had a load of missed calls from you."

His breath came down the line. "Someone's leaked your name and told the press you're working with us on the case. I'm sorry."

"Oh." Maybe that was why those men had come after her.

"What are you doing out and about at this time anyway?" Shawn asked. "I thought we told you to go home and get some rest."

"I know, but I couldn't do it. I did try, I promise, but all I kept doing was going back to the livestream. How can I sleep when I know someone out there needs my help and their clock is quite literally ticking down?"

"I understand," he said.

"Do you think they know where I live? Will Mum be okay?"

A wave of guilt washed over her. Had she put her mother's life in danger by getting involved? Her mum was her world, and she'd never forgive herself if something terrible happened.

"Maybe I should go back," she wondered.

"I'll send a car over there as well," Shawn said, "keep an eye on the house. Those two men were most likely just being opportunist dicks—they saw you and recognised you and decided to act like arseholes."

"I'm not sure. It felt like they were waiting for me..."

"How would they have known you were going to leave the house at this time of night?"

He had a point. She might be being too paranoid, but it was hardly surprising, considering what was going on. She hadn't thought to tell him about the two men who'd come knocking for her yesterday either.

People were being held captive, their tortures broadcast to the public, and though she knew she wasn't the only one responsible for trying to find them, she couldn't pretend like the whole thing hadn't unnerved her.

Chapter Twenty-Eight

S hawn ended the call, and Erica stared at him, waiting to be filled in. He told her what Jasmin had said.

"She sounded pretty shaken," he finished.

"Jesus Christ." She shook her head at herself. "I knew we shouldn't have brought her into this. She's just a kid."

"No, she isn't. She's an adult, and she won't appreciate you calling her a kid."

"Even so, what if she'd been hurt? I'd never have forgiven myself. Who the hell was it who leaked her name? Do you really think it might have been someone in the office?"

"It's more likely one of the reporters snapped pictures of her as she was coming to and from the office and did a bit of background research and put two and two together."

"I hope you're right. I don't like to think we can't trust one of our own. Where was she going?"

"Coming back into the office. She couldn't sleep and wanted to help."

Erica understood. She wouldn't have been able to sleep either, though she desperately needed some rest. How was it possible to rest when people's lives were quite literally on a timer? No one had confirmed the victims' deaths were the thing being counted down to, but it made sense. What else was likely to happen? She was glad Poppy was away at her residential so at least she didn't have to worry about childcare.

The thought of her daughter elicited a pang of longing. Though she'd appreciated having the freedom to work when she'd needed over these past few days, she desperately missed

Poppy's easy laughter and chatter. Spending time with her was the ultimate escapism. No one else took her mind off work in the same way Poppy did.

Both Erica and Shawn went out to the front of the building to wait for Jasmin's taxi.

It was night now, and though far from quiet, the city still had the sense of solitude that came from the biggest portion being asleep.

She fought a constant tug telling her to pull out her phone and check on the victims. She'd never been someone who was addicted to social media, but she was starting to understand the urge. Right now, she needed to focus on Jasmin. There was a possibility the men who'd attacked her were involved in the kidnapping of the victims, and if so, they might be able to find them and interrogate them. They had a reason to arrest them, since they'd assaulted Jasmin.

The lights of the black cab appeared, and Jasmin tapped her phone to pay the fare, and climbed out.

Shawn went into big cousin mode, putting his arm around her shoulders.

"You okay, Jasmin?" Erica asked her.

"Yeah, I'm not hurt or anything. Just a bit shaken up."

"Let's get you inside," Shawn said.

They ushered her through the office and sat her at Shawn's desk.

"Do you want something to drink?" Erica asked her. "Water, or tea, or coffee?"

Jasmin gave a rueful smile. "I don't suppose you've got anything stronger?"

"Not in the office, no."

Shawn jerked his head towards their boss's door. "What about in Gibbs' office? I bet he's got a bottle of something hidden in the filing cabinet."

Erica arched her eyebrows. "You really want to go rifling through his stuff?"

"Well...no."

"Water will be fine, thanks," Jasmin said.

"We're going to need to take a statement from you," Shawn said, "and take some scrapings from beneath your nails and swabs from your skin. We might get a DNA hit on those arseholes."

Jas nodded. "Whatever you need."

Shawn said. "I've sent a response car to the area, see if there's any sign of the two men, but they haven't spotted anyone."

Jas shivered. "They're probably long gone, though it might be worth checking in at A and E. I might have broken one of their noses."

Erica regarded her with a new appreciation. "Is that right?"

"Yeah, I headbutted him. I heard something go crunch."

"Definitely put that in the description then," Shawn said. "A bloodied nose and most likely two black eyes to boot. You've most likely got at least one of their DNA on you. You need to tell us everything that happened, every detail, no matter how small."

"They said they thought the victims should die," Jas said. "That they deserve what's happening to them because they're wealthy."

Erica shook her head. "No one deserves this. There's a good chance they have nothing to do with the actual people responsible for this. They could be two of the millions of people who've been watching what's been happening online."

Jasmin didn't seem convinced. "Or it could be them, and they saw I was poking around in their code and were worried I was getting too close. If that's the case then it's a good thing. It means I frightened them. They're worried I'm going to crack it and find out where they are."

"Someone leaked your name and photo," Shawn said. "We don't know who. The people who attacked you could be anyone."

Erica gave her a sympathetic smile. "The people who snatched the victims are professionals, Jasmin. They don't make mistakes, or at least they haven't so far. They're not going to risk screwing up and getting seen in order to take you out of the picture. I can't see them letting you get away either. If it had been the same people, you'd probably have found yourself locked up in one of those rooms as well."

"Maybe they weren't prepared this time," the girl suggested. "They hadn't been expecting me to get so close. Or they hadn't been expecting me at all. They'd planned for the others, but I was a curveball."

"Don't worry," Shawn reassured her. "We're going to do everything we can to find the men who attacked you, even if they're not the ones we're looking for. I understand that you might be nervous about going home now."

Jasmin set her jaw. "I'm not going home. I'm staying here until this is all over."

"You don't have to do that. You can walk away now," Erica told her. "You won't be thought of any different here if you do."

Jasmin pressed her lips together and shook her head. "What would be the point if I did? My name is already out there."

"Someone might be trying to frighten you off. If they think they've done that, then there's a chance they'll leave you alone."

Jasmin raised her eyebrows. "Do these seem like people who'll be content with leaving someone alone?"

Erica wished she'd trusted her gut and not got the girl involved. That she was a part of Shawn's extended family also worried her. What if these people learned that Jas also had a second cousin who was a detective working on the case? They might not limit who they were coming after to Jasmin. It made Erica sick to her stomach to think of any harm coming to any of them, but especially Shawn.

If he was torn from her life, she genuinely didn't think she was strong enough to go through losing him.

"Honestly, Jasmin," she said, "I really don't know."

Jas lifted her chin and put back her shoulders. "Then that's why I want to stay and help. If there's even the slightest chance of me helping to put these sick sons of bitches behind bars and saving those poor people, then that's exactly what I'm going to do."

A wave of pride for this young woman, whom Erica barely even knew, swept over her. It took some serious balls to face up to a threat like this.

"We'll get that car stationed outside your home," Erica reassured her. "No one will get anywhere near your mother."

"Thanks. Now, I've drunk three cans of Monster, one after the other, and I probably won't sleep for a week, so put me to work."

Erica remembered how it had felt to be nineteen. A strange combination of confidence and invincibility, combined with an insecurity and a desperate need to find your place in the world. She wouldn't want to go back to those times. However hard things seemed to be on occasion now, she knew exactly who she was and her reason for existing.

Shawn smiled at her. "First let's take those swabs and get your statement."

Erica left them to it.

Karl Hartley caught up with her. Like many of the others, he'd also stayed overnight to help.

"What's she doing back in the office?" he asked.

Erica explained what had happened. "Shawn's taking a statement now."

Karl's expression pinched. "You don't think that this is a huge distraction from what we're supposed to be working on?"

"Not necessarily. Think about it. If someone doesn't want Jasmin working on the case, maybe it's because they're worried she'll uncover something that they don't want her to find."

"You think they might be connected?"

"They specifically mentioned the case when they attacked her, so we can't pretend like it's not a possibility. Right now, we have so few leads, we can't afford to give any of them up, even if they seem tenuous."

"And if they're not connected?"

She shrugged. "Then we'll have taken two arseholes off the street who think it's okay to beat up a teenage girl. Win-win." Something struck her. "Actually, she might be the perfect witness."

• • • •

"JASMIN, DO YOU RECOGNISE any of these people?"

Erica had laid out a selection of photographs. Some were those whose names had been mentioned by the head of the organisation, and others were headshots used to ensure it wasn't only a happy accident if Jasmin happened to ID men from The Climate Uprising.

Jasmin glanced over at her. "Remember it was dark, and one of them came up behind me. I'm not sure what help I'm going to be."

"Try," Erica encouraged her. "If you can't ID any of them, it's fine. We'll figure this out another way."

Jas pressed her lips together and approached the table cautiously. It wasn't easy, being forced to face something that been a traumatic experience. Even if she didn't recognise any of them, just being asked to recollect what had happened, to try to picture their faces in her mind, could be triggering.

"Take your time," Erica told her.

She almost said 'there's no rush' but managed to bite her tongue. There was a rush, and all of them knew it. A clock was literally counting down.

"Can I pick up the photographs?" she asked.

"Of course."

As though she was worried the pictures themselves might come to life and attack her, Jas reached out a shaking hand and picked up the closest photograph. She stared at it for a few seconds, then shook her head and put it back down.

"Definitely not that one."

She moved on to the next and repeated the process. She bit her lower lip. "It's not this one either." She put down that one and selected the third. "I don't know if I'm—"

Jas fell silent as she stared down at the picture. She lifted it, as though she was trying to see the face from a different angle.

Erica remained quiet, giving her time to process what she was seeing.

"This was one of the men," Jas said, handing Erica the photograph.

"You're sure?"

She nodded. "Yes."

"One hundred percent? You said it was dark..."

"I know, but this is definitely him. I didn't think I was going to recognise him, but the second I saw that photo it was like someone had punched me in the gut. It's definitely him."

Erica jerked her chin at the remaining photographs. "What about the other one?"

"He came at me from behind, so I'm not sure, but I'll keep looking."

Jasmin continued to go through the pictures. She stopped on one.

"I think this is him. He was tall and skinny, but strong. He had on gold jewellery—a thick gold necklace and a gold ring, too."

"A wedding ring?"

"I don't think so, but it might have been."

Erica remembered the CCTV footage from the building Catherine had been abducted from. The driver of the van had also been wearing a gold ring. Unfortunately, that wasn't unusual, and it wouldn't be enough to prove that he'd been the one to snatch Catherine—if, in fact, he was guilty.

"Those details are really helpful, Jas. Thank you. We're already tracking these two down and then we can start asking some questions."

Her identification of the second man might not be strong enough to hold up in court, especially considering it was dark and he'd caught her from behind. A decent defence would easily argue that she could be mistaken. The first one, however, she seemed pretty certain about.

Erica picked up the photographs. The first man she'd ID'd was Tommy Biel. The second one, who she'd headbutted, was Gordie Carol.

Both were members of The Climate Uprising.

Chapter Twenty-Nine

E rica took in the corridor outside the interview rooms. In one room was Gordie Carol, and in the other was Tommy Biel.

She punched in the code to access the room and stepped inside.

The young man slouched behind the table had two black eyes, and his nose didn't appear to be on straight. Erica almost wanted to go and shake Jas's hand. While she didn't believe in violence, sometimes it was necessary. If Jasmin hadn't defended herself, Erica didn't want to imagine what would have happened to her. Maybe she'd have been another livestream by the end of the day?

These two meatheads didn't seem to have it in them to run such a complicated crime, though. Neither of them had any kind of tech background, and while that didn't immediately rule them out, since plenty of people were self-taught these days, they didn't seem bright enough. Perhaps it was all an act, and beneath the dull eyes and slack lower lip there was a man of sharp intelligence, but she didn't think so. She liked to think she was a good judge of character, but it wouldn't be the first time she'd been proven wrong. There had been plenty of occasions where she'd made a mistake about something, had thought they were something they weren't. This might be another situation like that.

Erica didn't sit initially. "Hello, Mr Carol. I'm DI Swift. Do you understand why you've been brought in?"

He curled his lip in a sneer. "Under some bullshit charge. I haven't done anything wrong."

"We'll see about that. Would you like to have a solicitor present before we speak? If you can't afford one, we can allocate you one."

"I don't need a fucking solicitor. I'm innocent."

She took a seat and went through the process of starting the recording and announcing the location, date, and who was in the room, and then read him his rights once more and that he'd rejected his rights to a solicitor being present. If this went to court, she wanted to make sure everything had been done by the book. She didn't want some slimy defence solicitor getting him off the hook because of a technicality.

"Mr Carol, how long have you been a member of The Climate Uprising?"

"I dunno. Couple of years."

"Do you feel enough is being done to tackle climate change?"

"Right now, it is. Whoever's kidnapped those people is doing a good job, in my opinion."

Erica paused and sat back. "Want to tell me what happened to your face, Gordie?"

He pursed his lips. "I walked into a door."

"Yeah? When did that happen?"

He shrugged. "The other night."

"Really? It looks fresh to me. The bruising hasn't started to change colour yet. Did you get any medical attention for it? Go to the doctor or the hospital?"

"No. It's fine."

"I'm not a medic, but your nose appears to be broken, Gordie. It must hurt like hell. Why didn't you go to the hospital when it happened?"

"I already told you why."

"Or is the reason actually because you didn't hurt your nose by walking into a door, but because you tried to assault a young woman and she head butted you?"

He scoffed. "No girl did this."

"That's not what our witness says. She also picked you and Tommy quite confidently out of a lineup of photographs."

"That bitch is lying."

"Why would she do that?"

He didn't answer but let his shoulders rise and fall.

"For the purpose of the tape," Erica said, "Mr Carol has just shrugged." She fell quiet again, giving him the opportunity to fill in the silence with information of his own, but when he said nothing, she continued. "Where were you shortly after eleven last night?

"I dunno. In bed, probably."

She pulled up a screenshot from CCTV near the area where Jasmin had been attacked. It was grainy but was clearly a shot of Gordie and Tommy standing in the street together. The time stamp was a few minutes after eleven.

She showed him the image. "That's strange, because if you were in bed, then it would seem you have the ability to be in two places at once. This shot was taken a few streets away from where the victim lives and was attacked shortly afterwards."

He stared at the image and then glanced away. "That's not me."

Erica couldn't help herself, she laughed at the absurdity of his comment. "Are you about to tell me you have a twin?"

"No."

"Then come on, Gordie. You know you're not going to get away with this. The witness can ID you, you have visible injuries that match her version of events, and there's CCTV that puts you at the scene. Here's where my mind is going with things, though. According to the witness, you said the people who've been kidnapped, the ones who are being broadcast over the internet—I'm sure you know exactly who I mean—deserved to die, and if someone went to these lengths to stop someone who was trying to help those people, then maybe they know more about what's happening to them than they're letting on."

He pinched his lips, clearly wrestling with himself. Then he let out a sigh and sat forwards, planting his forearms on the table.

"Look, we might have tried to scare the girl off, but we didn't have anything to do with kidnapping those people or what's happening to them now. I have no idea where they're being held."

She arched her eyebrows. "But you found out where Jasmin Webb lives? That wasn't so hard."

He threw up his hands. "That's 'cause it's all over the fucking internet. As is the fact she's working with the police to try and find these people."

"And you decided to try and scare her off doing that. Why?"

"Because we meant what we said about them not deserving to live. Do you know who these people are? What kind of havoc they want to wreak on the environment?"

"Richard Morrisey hasn't done anything to harm the environment."

He snorted. "Yeah, right. He's as bad as his wife. She might be the politician, but I guarantee he's whispering in her ear, and that's before we even get started on the huge four-by-four he drives just to do the school run and the multiple foreign holidays a year. That money he's living on has been earned by sacrificing our environment."

Erica thought of something and raised a finger. "Hang on a minute, didn't Nancy Morrisey support a wind farm being built out on the North Sea instead of allowing for more drilling? How does that make her bad?"

"Okay, so she did one decent thing, and that's only because of the pressure that's been on her because of groups like us. What's it called..." he sought for the right word... "virtue signalling. She doesn't actually give a shit."

"So you punished her husband because the steps she took in the right direction weren't good enough?" Erica couldn't hide the disbelief from her tone.

He thumped his fist down on the table. "No! We didn't do anything. Okay, we might have tried to scare Jasmin Webb a little, but that was all."

She folded her hands on the table and took a breath. "You do see how this looks, don't you, Gordie? And if your friend in the other interview room is talking, you understand how bad this will be for you when it comes to a trial."

His jaw dropped. "If Tommy is talking, I have no idea what he's saying, because I swear to you that I had nothing to do with what's going on with those people on the internet. If Tommy did, then that's got nothing to do with me either. I'm fucking innocent!"

"You attacked a nineteen-year-old girl. You waited outside her house and stalked her. Does that really sound like the actions of an innocent man?"

He had the decency to at least appear awkward, his lips pinching as he glanced down at the table. "Yeah, okay, I'll admit that wasn't my finest moment, but that still doesn't mean I'm guilty of the other thing."

"What about the times of the kidnappings," she said. "Where were you on those times and dates?" She ran through each of them individually.

"I don't fucking know."

"You're going to need to remember."

"That early in the morning?" He shrugged. "Probably in bed, asleep. I don't do early mornings."

"Were you with anyone who can verify that?" she asked.

"I dunno. My housemates, probably."

"You live with other people?"

He snorted. "Yeah, of course I do. Have you seen London rental prices lately? We can barely afford a whole room of our own."

"I'm going to need the names of those housemates. Are they a part of The Climate Uprising, too?"

"Nah, they don't give a shit about the environment. I'm lucky if I can get them to put a bottle in the recycling bin."

Erica took out her phone and brought up the live feeds of the victims. Someone had created a channel where it was possible to see all three of the livestreams on one page, so she no longer had to flick between them. It was like the world's most horrifying Zoom call. The counter continued to tick its way down to zero.

"Time is literally running out," she said. "Look at these videos. These are people with their own lives. They don't deserve this. No one deserves this."

Frustratingly, he shrugged again. The sight of the tortured victims seemed to have no effect on him.

Erica tried a different angle. "Richard Morrisey has two children. They're ten and twelve years old. You say you're fighting for the futures of our children, but what kind of future do these two little kids have in store for them if they lose their father in such a graphic way?"

"There are children all over the world who are suffering from far worse because of climate change. Millions of children who are starving to death because global warming means they have no rain and their families' crops are failing. Why should these two children be more important? Is it because they're white and from a good background? The sort of children we're supposed to care about when so many others are forgotten?"

Erica could tell she wasn't getting anywhere.

She exhaled a breath and spoke for the tape. "Interview ended at one twenty-six a.m.," she said and hit the pause button. "I think it's time for a break, don't you?"

"You need to let me go."

"You're under arrest for assault. You're not going anywhere."

"But I'm not under arrest for what's happening to those people. If you had proof, you'd have got me for that as well. So don't try to fool me that Tommy is talking when he clearly isn't."

She didn't reply but got to her feet. "I'm taking a break. I'll get you a coffee, shall I? Or are coffee beans bad for the environment as well?"

"Actually, now you mention it—"

She didn't wait long enough to hear the rest of his reply. No one was taking her coffee from her.

She left the interview room and went to see how Shawn was doing next door. She knocked lightly and then stuck her head in. "Take a break?"

"For the benefit of the tape, DI Swift has entered the room," Shawn said.

He glanced across the table to where Tommy Biel was sitting, his head bent over the table.

"Sounds good. What do you think, Tommy?"

Tommy seemed to have gone to the same school of nonchalance as his mate, as he just shrugged as well.

She retreated again to give Shawn a moment to round things off, then he stepped out to join her in the corridor.

"How are you getting on?" she asked him.

"He's admitted to attacking Jas but is insisting he doesn't know anything about the kidnappings or the videos. He claims he has no idea where those people are being held."

"I'm getting a similar story. It's not as though he sounds exactly remorseful about what they're going through, however."

"We're running out of time."

She wanted to tell him that it hadn't escaped her notice but bit her tongue. Her stress levels were running high.

If she didn't find these people, and their deaths were screened live over the internet, everyone was going to know that she'd failed them. Their blood would be on her hands. Maybe it was selfish to even have that concern in the back of her mind when people would be losing their lives, but it was hard not to think about how this was going to impact her and her family. She was the SIO, and if they died, inquiries into how she'd conducted the investigation would be held. This was already an extremely high-profile case. If she was accused of messing up somewhere along the way, everyone would hear about it. She didn't want Poppy to go into school and have to face taunts from other pupils, or for her sister to face backlash simply for being related to her.

Shawn folded his arms across his chest. "What if they're telling the truth? Maybe they didn't have anything to do with the kidnappings."

"Gordie claims to have been home at the time of the kidnappings, that his housemates can provide an alibi, but obviously we haven't had the chance to check up on that yet."

"And if both of them have proven alibis for the kidnappings?" He raised his eyebrows. "What then?"

"It doesn't mean The Climate Uprising aren't involved, just that it wasn't those specific members who were responsible. We still know they attacked Jas. Maybe it was some other members who did the kidnapping. The profile of whoever is behind this is someone who knows their tech, and I don't think either of those two fit that. I mean, unless they're extremely good actors, it's not as though they're the smartest pair, are they?"

"Agreed," Shawn said. "Someone with some serious smarts must be responsible for coordinating all of this and setting up a feed that even Counter Terrorism haven't been able to crack."

She considered this. "This kind of thing takes money, too, and these two definitely don't have that."

"Does that mean they don't know anything, though? What about offering them some kind of deal. We'll lessen the charges on them if they give us information on who might be behind this."

She blew out a breath. "And if they continue to claim not to know?"

"Then they're still both charged with assault." Shawn clucked his tongue against his teeth. "I think we need to take another look at the membership list. Are any of them trained in IT or anything like that?"

Erica tore her hand through her hair and paced the corridor. "We don't have time for this! We have hours, that's it, and then God only knows what's going to happen to those poor people. Have you seen Richard recently? If the water gets much higher the next time it rises, he will drown, there's no question about it."

"The water's always gone down before it's reached that point," Shawn said.

"Yes, but that was when he had more time on the clock. Each time the room has filled with water, it's been a little higher each time. When it rises this morning, it'll be high enough that he'll drown." Something dinged inside her head, and she stopped pacing and drew a breath. Her mind whirred. "Hang on a minute, there's a pattern to it, right? Water goes up and down, but it's not at the same time of day, at least not quite. It's a little later each time, right?"

"Yeah, seems that way."

Erica felt like smacking herself in the head. Why hadn't she realised it before? "On the second morning, it was at its highest at about five a.m., but the clock ends just after six this morning. Why is that?" She took out her phone and typed in a search. "The times the room has been flooded correspond with the times of the high tide."

"Shit, you're right."

"And why is the water going to be at its highest? Isn't tonight a full moon? We know Richard can't have been taken far enough away to have reached the ocean. He must be somewhere closer. How far along is the Thames River tidal?"

"I have no idea," Shawn said, but he took out his phone to Google it. "There's almost a hundred miles of it being tidal, but of course the tidal part is strongest the closer we get to the sea."

"Okay, and we know that he must be within a certain range of his home because the kidnapper simply didn't have time to take him farther."

"You think he's somewhere on the Thames?"

Erica fixed Shawn in her gaze. "He has to be. Get a map. Let's mark out potential locations where Richard might be being held. It would need to be away from the general public, somewhere on the riverbank, within an hour's drive of his home."

Shawn nodded. "I'll get the team onto it right away."

Chapter Thirty

T he sun would be up soon.

They were on their final day, and, according to the clock, the victims only had two hours to live.

Erica scrubbed her eyes. They were sore and gritty. She'd put her head down at her desk for a couple of hours and had woken with a smear of drool and the print of her paperwork on her cheek.

As had become her habit, the first thing she did upon opening her eyes was check the livestreams. Water was entering Richard's room again, and was already up to his waist, Catherine lay on the floor of the sauna and didn't appear to be moving, and Hector was so weak he could barely lift his hand.

Something had changed.

The voice that had played over the video feeds and into the rooms was speaking again.

Shawn approached her desk. "Have you heard what he's saying now?"

"I just turned it on."

Erica gave the computer her full attention.

"This is horrifying to you, isn't it?" the male voice said. "One man about to drown...a woman roasting alive...another starving to death. The police are scrambling to try to save these people, and to try to catch us, but why? What's so special about these three human beings that all this time and energy and resources are being put into trying to save them when we turn our backs on thousands of people dying every day in these exact same ways? Flooding is wiping out people's homes and taking them with it, and no one cares. The rise in temperature is causing forest fires, which devastate the wildlife and burn people alive, but still, no one cares. Famine sees millions starving to death, even small children, and yet we do nothing.

"So why is the idea of these three people dying the same way so horrifying to you? If I told you that if you never took another flight to a foreign country, I would save this woman's life, would you agree to it? Or would you put your foreign holidays above saving her? If I told you that you could stop eating meat, and I would let this man go, would you do it? It's not such a hardship, is it, to save another's life? If I asked you to give up your car, and I'd feed this poor man, would you wave your vehicle goodbye?

"I'd like to think it would be an easy decision for most of you watching right now. That you'd put another human's life above your own comfort and way of life. So why is it so hard to do it for all those people who you're not watching on the internet, but who are dying all the same?"

Erica glanced at Shawn. "Is that what he wants? For us to somehow make a promise that those things will happen, and he'll release the captives?"

"How can we? We have no way of communicating with him."

"We do. In the comments of his post."

"Okay, so everyone promises to give up those things, but how would he know they were keeping to it? Someone could promise to give up international flights and then turn around tomorrow and book an all-inclusive holiday in Mauritius."

Erica shook her head. "I don't know, but isn't it worth a try?"

"Would you be able to do it?" Shawn asked. "I mean, he kind of has a point, doesn't he?"

She considered this. "I guess I could eat less meat, and I never go abroad anyway, but how can we give up our cars? In our line of work? What are we supposed to do, chase criminals down on our pushbikes? Besides, it's all nice in theory, but life doesn't work like that. Say if we all give up meat tomorrow, what would happen to all the farmers and their livelihoods? What would happen to all the animals? No one is going to look after them if they don't bring in any money. No one would be able to afford to feed them or pay for vet visits or anything like that, so they'd all have to be shot. Is that what this arsehole is trying to achieve?"

Shawn gestured at the screen. "Check out the comments. Whatever he's doing, it's working."

Sure enough, people were commenting.

<Please save her. I'll stop eating meat.>

<I've been a vegetarian for years. That should count for something.>

<I'll give up my foreign holidays. Don't let anyone else die.>

Mixed in with those were the usual vitriol from the trolls.

<I want to watch the bitch die. Fry her brains.>

<Who gives a shit about any of those people? No one's taking my bacon from me.>

<We're all going to die anyway. Might as well enjoy ourselves while we're here.>

Erica glanced up at Shawn. "I guess I'd better respond. I'm not making any promises, though." She remembered Tina's statement. "We don't negotiate with terrorists."

Her fingers flew across the keys.

< This is the Met Police. We ask that you let the victims go unharmed. Killing them is only going to undermine what you're trying to achieve. If you want the public on your side, show compassion. >

She sat back and rubbed her hands over her face. "It's not going to be enough."

Shawn put his hand on her shoulder and rubbed out the knots from sleeping at her desk. "It's something."

"It's not enough," she repeated.

The truth was that they were going to be too late. They were doing everything they could, but they still hadn't narrowed it down to any individuals. Right now, everything they had on The Climate Uprising's involvement was circumstantial. Yes, they might have been hassling Nancy Morrisey, and two of their members had attacked Jasmin, but it still didn't mean they were the ones responsible.

Just as she'd felt like she'd given up, an overexcited Jasmin rushed up to her desk.

"I think I might have cracked it," Jas cried. "I got through the software that was switching the locations and used a malware to corrupt it, and from there I was able to narrow down where the very first signal originated from."

Erica straightened. "Tell me."

"You understand that this information can't provide an exact address—only a postal code?"

"I understand. Where is it?"

"It's the postal code for Woolwich. As well as that, I've been able to look up the associated hostname and the organisation that owns the IP. Here's where it gets interesting. The company that owns it is one that belongs to Hector Townsend."

"A company based in Woolwich?"

"Not exactly," Jas continued. "Hector Townsend is a millionaire, with numerous investments and businesses, right? As well as working for the oil industry, he also buys up failing businesses and converts them into profitable ones. Sometimes, this includes the land the businesses are located on."

"Okay," Erica said impatiently. "What point are you trying to make here? In case you hadn't noticed, we're short on time."

She handed Erica a tablet that had a map of the area on the screen. "One of the company addresses is located on the Woolwich dry docks. It was used for boat maintenance, but it's been closed for several years now. It would appear Hector was trying to get planning for building a block of exclusive apartments, except the reports came back that the land wasn't suitable for construction. Want to take a guess why?"

"Why?" Erica asked, playing along.

"Because it's prone to flooding."

"Like when there's a particularly high tide?"

Jas nodded. "Exactly."

"Shit." Erica turned to Shawn. "Do we know if anyone thought to search the property when Hector first went missing?"

He shook his head. "Not as far as I'm aware. They had no reason to think he might be there. It's an abandoned site."

"At least that's what it looks like from the surface."

Erica checked the time. It was less than two hours left until it ran out.

"Let's get a team over there. If there's any chance we find Richard there, then we might also find something that'll help us find the others."

"You don't think they're all going to be kept in the same location?"

"Honestly, I have no idea at this point. Let's hope so, but we can't put our money on it."

It was going to take them thirty minutes to get to the location, and they didn't have that time to waste. Erica put in calls to any units around the Woolwich area who could be on site asap. Everyone knew about what was happening, so they didn't need a full briefing.

"Whoever's taken them could be dangerous," Shawn said. "Let's request an Armed Response Team."

"We need paramedics on standby, too. The victims are all going to need medical attention after what they've been through."

Erica's stomach flipped with nerves. "That's assuming we get to them in time."

"Well, yes. Let's hope so."

Erica quickly filled Gibbs in on what they'd learned. "We don't know for sure that we're going to find Richard or the others at the location, but it's the best lead we've got."

"That girl did a good job," he said.

"Yes, she did, didn't she? We're lucky we had her working with us."

Shawn had been right to bring her in.

• • • •

FOR ONCE, ERICA LET Shawn drive. She wanted to watch the livestreams in case anything changed. Would the person—or persons—behind this know they were coming? Had anything changed on their end that would tell them they'd been hit by a malware and the VPN no longer worked? If so, they might try to move the victims, or, even worse, decide to speed up the process and kill them before the clock ran down.

It was Catherine Taura she worried about most. The woman hadn't moved in some time.

Was the temperature increasing in the sauna? If that's how they planned on killing her, it would make sense. If she wasn't at the Woolwich site, they wouldn't have time to find her and save her as well.

It didn't bear thinking about.

At least they had something to go on. The possibility they might be wrong weighed heavily on her shoulders. The whole country was watching right now—maybe even the world. She didn't even want to think about how the public would react if these three people died live online while she'd sent her team to the wrong location. There would be an outcry. Was that what these protestors wanted?

By the time Erica and Shawn, and the rest of the team arrived at the site, the investigation was already well underway. An Armed Response Unit had also arrived, and uniformed officers were closing off the roads surrounding the site. Luckily, the area they were in wasn't a residential one, so they didn't have to worry about locals having a bird's eye view on what was going on.

It was still painfully early, the sun breaching the horizon. The brackish scent of the Thames reached her nose, and, to her left, the murky river carried a couple of boats.

Would people instantly realise that this operation had to do with the livestream? She was surprised no reporters had followed them here, but she expected they'd get wind that something was going down soon enough.

She hurried over to one of the sergeants who'd been first on scene and was helping to run the operation.

"We've got officers searching the site," he said. "It's large, though, and on several different levels. It doesn't look like much, but most of it's hidden from ground view. Believe it or not, this place used to be used by smugglers after the First World War."

Erica glanced out towards the water. It made sense that wherever Richard was being held, it would be closest to the river. "How do I get down there?"

"Inside that building," the sergeant said, "there are concrete steps going down. You'll find yourself in a corridor. Be careful, we haven't had the chance to cover all of it yet."

"Thanks."

Erica pulled on a protective vest, in case the perpetrator was armed. Shawn did the same. They joined the officers already preparing to enter.

"We have the schematics for this place. It's like a rabbit warren, so we're going to need to split up to get it covered as quickly as possible. There might be some parts that haven't been featured on the plan, but until we see for ourselves, we won't know."

Aware she might not get any mobile reception below ground level, she quickly checked her phone. The water was up to Richard's chin now, his head tilted back to keep his nose and mouth above the surface. Because he was chained to the chair, he couldn't rise any farther. If they didn't get in there soon, he would drown.

She followed the other officers into the bare concrete structure of the abandoned building and headed down.

The air smelled damp, and darker patches on the floor and walls indicated where the proximity to the Thames had made itself known. No wonder they hadn't got permission to build residential homes. Like many areas, water had been drained from this spot to create the dry docks and the surrounding areas, but whoever had done so hadn't done a good enough job. Maybe it could be fixable, but it would be at a huge expense.

They took a left, towards the river. Strip lights in the ceiling lit the way.

"He kept the power going," Erica said, half to herself, keeping her voice low in case anyone was close enough to hear. "The internet connection, too."

Shawn glanced her way. "What?"

"The site was no use to him, but Hector Townsend kept paying for power to this place."

"I guess when you're super rich, you don't need to worry about getting the bills each month."

Erica wasn't so sure about that. Some of the wealthiest people Erica had come across were also the tightest. They had millions in the bank but would fight about whose turn it was to buy the coffee or would haggle a trader down to the cheapest price they could. People who had millions didn't have millions because they loved to spend. They tended to be hoarders of their wealth.

A shout came from one of the officers ahead of them. "We've found something."

Erica and Shawn exchanged a glance and picked up their pace.

At the end of one of the corridors was a heavy metal door.

"Looks like it's sealed," the officer said. "Soldered shut. There's no lock or door handle."

"Shit," Erica cursed. "We're going to need some equipment." She thought for a moment. There's a building site next door. See if they've got anything we can use."

"I'll go back," the officer said, brushing past them to go back to ground level and find what was needed.

Erica took out her phone to check the livestream.

"Can you see what's going on?" Shawn asked.

She shook her head. "The screen's frozen. I don't have any signal down here." She moved closer to the door, pressed her ear up against it. "Are you in there, Richard?"

"Can you hear that?" Shawn said. "It sounds like splashing."

Something else occurred to her. "Wait! There's electricity and water down here. That's not a good combination. The camera and lights must be plugged into something, but since he hasn't been electrocuted already, any power source must have been run high in the walls, or maybe even the ceiling. What if the way he's going to die isn't by drowning, but because the water is going to hit an electrical socket and the electricity is going to kill him. We can't risk being in the water if that happens. When we open the door, the water will flood through the corridors. It'll kill us, too."

Erica turned back to the rest of the team. "Does anyone know how to shut the power off to this place? Can someone get onto the electricity board?"

"If we shut the power off," Shawn said, "it'll kill the cameras. There won't be any more livestreams, but we'll also lose our connection to the victims."

"Maybe that'll be a good thing. The rest of the show won't be viewed by all those people online either."

"Okay, good. Let's do it then."

She checked her watch. Less than an hour remained.

It felt like a frustratingly long amount of time had passed, but finally, the officer returned with a cordless angle grinder and a set of protective goggles.

"Give me some space," he said. "Step back!"

Cutting metal would send little shards flying everywhere and could injure someone.

He got to work, starting at the top-right corner of the door and working his way downwards. Water trickled from the areas that he'd cut, pooling around their feet. The pressure of the water behind the door would be alleviated as the water ran out into the corridor, but there was also the chance the soldering that had been done to keep the door shut and the water inside would give, and they'd be hit by the force of a metal door and all the water behind it.

He kept going.

Erica's heart was in her throat. Would Richard still be alive by the time they reached him?

The officer had cut two thirds of the way around the door when it buckled. Water flooded through the corridor, almost knocking Erica and the other officers around her off their feet. She clutched at Shawn's arm, her other hand finding the solid concrete wall, and they managed to keep their balance. She was taken back to a previous case where an amputee almost drowned after punching a hole in the side of the boat she'd been kept captive on. She could have drowned that day.

Beams of torchlight lit the room beyond to reveal Richard Morrisey, soaking wet, still chained to the chair but very much alive.

"Thank God," he sobbed. "Oh, thank God. I thought I was going to die."

"Someone get him out of those chains," Erica said. "Use the angle grinder again if you need to." She turned her attention to the victim. "It's okay, Richard. You're safe now." She glanced behind her. "We need paramedics!"

The officers worked to free him, but he was too weak to stand.

"Do you know where the other victims are being held?" Erica asked him. "Have you heard any noises from anyone else?"

Pure confusion crossed his face. "Other victims? What other victims?"

He clearly didn't know anything.

She left him in the capable hands of the other officers and the paramedics. They might have saved Richard, but there were two other victims to find. When she was close enough to ground level, she checked her phone again.

With the power cut, the screens had gone blank.

Erica faced Shawn.

"They have to be here somewhere, or at least close enough by to be affected by us cutting the power. We need to keep searching."

Someone shouted her name, and she turned to find a young female officer trying to get her attention.

"DI Swift, we've found the sauna on the other side of the property. We're trying to get inside it now."

"Is Catherine still alive?"

"Unsure right now. I don't think it's still being heated due to the power being out, but it's still going to retain the heat it had."

"Dammit."

She broke into a run, her shoes squelching, as she followed the other officers back down through the building. This place was a warren of bunker-style rooms and concrete tunnels. She pictured the smugglers back in the day bringing the crates of booze up the Thames and then squirreling it away here until they'd found a buyer. Other than a few modern upgrades, it didn't feel as though much had changed.

As there was no longer power to the place, they needed to use torches now to light the way.

At the end of one of the corridors, the light wood of the sauna came into view in the torchlight. The sight of it was so bizarre, out of place, like a mirage. There was no doubt this had been purposefully built.

Beyond the steamy and bloodied glass of the door, the woman's body lay curled on the floor. Were they too late?

"Catherine?" Erica shouted.

She didn't respond.

Shit. "We need to get in there. Now!"

There was no lock on the door. It seemed the actual door handle itself was broken, and that was what kept it shut. Someone got in there with a screwdriver and removed the whole door handle, so the door swung open.

"Jesus Christ," Erica muttered.

One of the paramedics was the first to reach her. "She's got no pulse." He raised his voice. "We need a crash kit." One of his colleagues hurried in to assist him.

Erica stayed back and let them do their work.

"Where's Hector? If the other two are here, then he must be, too."

"We're still searching, ma'am."

Finally, she got the word she'd been hoping for. They'd found Hector, too.

His door wasn't locked.

Whoever had been holding him captive this past month must have realised he was too weak to go anywhere. The smell in the room was overwhelming. There was a toilet, but it clearly hadn't been cleaned in some time. The state of the bed and the mattress wasn't pleasant either. She did her best not to allow her shock and revulsion show on her face. This man was nothing like the photographs and footage she'd seen online when she'd been researching him, the self-assured, confident man in the expensive suits, shaking hands with all the right people and delivering speeches in front of rooms of hundreds of people. He'd been reduced to a shell of himself.

"Mr Townsend? I'm with the police. We're here to help you."

He could barely move, he was so weak. What kind of monster had done this to these people?

"Do you know who did this to you?"

His voice was a faint rasp. "Those damned protestors. They're all crazy. It was those Climate Uprising people."

"I'm going to need more than that, Mr Townsend. Can you give me a name? Or even a description?"

But he shook his head.

How was it possible for him not to have seen anyone if he'd been kept down here all that time? Surely someone had been bringing him some kind of sustenance.

Bringing each of the victims to ground level was a big operation.

"This whole place is a crime scene," Erica said. "We need to get SOCO in asap and get it taped off."

The relief of finding the victims was overwhelming. She genuinely hadn't believed it was going to happen. Had whoever was behind this made a mistake by keeping them all in one place? Maybe it hadn't been possible to use separate locations. After all, this site was perfect for what they'd tried to achieve. If Hector had been harder to identify, they might never have known to come here. As it was, there was no one around the area who might have spotted something strange going on, no one close by enough to hear any cries for help. The room—that was really no more than a bunker—where Richard had been held was right on the waterline, and the other two rooms were also below ground level but far enough away from the water that the rising tide didn't affect them.

That it was Hector's property was genius, too. Of course, no progress could be made on the site with Hector missing.

One of the paramedics caught up to her.

"I'm sorry, but we were too late for Catherine Taura. We couldn't bring her back around. She must have fallen into a coma long before we got there."

Erica's heart sank. They hadn't made it in time, at least for Catherine.

"Thanks for letting me know. We're going to need to inform her next of kin, her husband."

The poor man. Imagine losing a partner that way, in front of an audience of hundreds of thousands, if not millions.

The Climate Uprising wouldn't have won themselves any fans.

Chapter Thirty-One

L ater, at the hospital, Erica and Shawn went to visit both the surviving victims.

They found Hector Townsend in a private room. He had been put on a drip but already seemed stronger, brighter. He was half sitting, propped up by numerous pillows.

"Mr Townsend," Erica said, "I understand it's still early days, but we need to talk to you, find out exactly what you remember."

"I don't remember much of the actual abduction, I'm afraid. One minute I was walking along my street, and the next I was being bundled into a white van, and then I must have blacked out. I woke up in that damned room."

"Did you see anyone in the time you were down there?"

"No. I haven't seen anyone since they took me. They shut me in there with supplies. But they never told me I needed to make them last all this time. I felt sure someone would have found me by now. I didn't know what their plan was. For the first couple of days, I ate what I wanted. I was frightened and bored, but then a voice came over a speaker, jeering, almost teasing me, and suggested that I might want to make what they'd given me last. That was when I realised I would be in here for some time. And that I needed to make what I had last me 'cause they might not give me any more."

"And they didn't?" she asked.

He lifted one thin arm. "Clearly not." He paused and said, "How are the other victims? You said there were more."

"The other man survived. Sadly, the woman didn't make it."

"She died?" The shock was clear on his face. "How?"

"Prolonged exposure to heat. We think a combination of dehydration and her heart giving out."

"There was water in the room, wasn't there? I mean, they left me water. Wouldn't they have done the same for her?"

"It was a different situation." She debated how much to tell him but then realised he would be shown the videos at some point. "She was locked in a sauna."

"But there's water in a sauna, isn't there? Why would she have ended up dehydrated?"

"Her body couldn't cope. We don't know what kind of underlying medical conditions she might have had as well. We'll know more once the post-mortem is carried out."

He seemed shell-shocked, no doubt putting himself in the poor woman's place. It could have been any of them, or all of them, if they hadn't been found when they had.

Erica continued. "In the room, you said it was the people behind The Climate Uprising who did this to you. What made you say that?"

"They told me that was who they were with. That I deserved what was happening to me because I'd been benefitting from plundering the earth, or some such nonsense as that."

"But they didn't show you any proof of that?"

He gave a weird, strangled kind of laugh. "I'd say keeping me in that room and almost starving me to death is proof enough. What about the other victims? Were they told the same?"

"Unfortunately, we never got the chance to ask Catherine anything, and Richard is still in shock, but it does seem someone acted without the knowledge of other members of the group, or possibly someone is just using the name."

It didn't matter that someone was using the name. It had got out now, and the general public and the media were running with it.

Would they ever find out exactly who was behind this? They had SOCO working the Woolwich location, so there was every chance they'd pick up on prints or DNA that they could match with someone on file, but their best bet would have been getting a description or even a name from one of the victims.

"I'm sorry I can't be of more help," Hector said.

• • • •

ERICA AND HER TEAM still had a lot of work ahead of them. Though they'd found the victims, they hadn't yet pinned down the culprits.

Though Hector was able to point a finger at the climate change activist group to be responsible, they had yet to nail it down to any one or more individuals.

In order to get the site set up, someone must have been coming and going for weeks before the abductions, if not longer. They were digging up any security footage from both the site and the surrounding area. Traffic cameras would be checked in case they picked up any repeated sightings of white vans coming to and from the location.

Trawling through weeks' worth of local traffic cameras and methodically ticking off each white van caught on camera was going to be slow, laborious work, but they had no choice.

Someone had built the sauna, but they had yet to find out who. If they were able to figure out who'd commissioned it, then they'd be able to follow the paper trail back to whoever was responsible.

Now they had a crime scene and witnesses, she doubted it would be long before they nailed someone for the crime. Whoever had killed Catherine Taura needed to pay.

Chapter Thirty-Two

Poppy was due to come home tomorrow.

After barely sleeping the previous night, Erica was able to get off early. She'd catch up on some sleep and then pick up some of Poppy's favourite food for when she got home.

Erica couldn't wait. After the chaos of the past few days, she longed for some normality.

Her phone rang, but she didn't recognise the number. "DI Swift," she answered.

A female voice. "Oh, hello. Is this Poppy Swift's mum?"

A chill ran across Erica's skin. "Yes, who is this?"

"My name's Dawn Farnum, and I'm one of the helpers down at the centre where the children are staying at the moment."

"Is everything okay? Is Poppy okay?"

The woman hesitated. "There's been an incident while they were caving. Some of the roof has had a small cave-in, and one of the leaders is stuck."

Despite herself, a small part of her relaxed at the knowledge they weren't calling about Poppy. "That's terrible. Is he okay?"

The person on the end of the line took a breath. "The emergency services and a specialist cave rescue team is working on freeing him, but the reason I'm contacting you directly is that five children are with him."

Her blood froze to ice in her veins. "What? What do you mean? They're still with him?"

"They were on their way out when the roof collapse happened, which means the children are currently trapped behind him. I'm afraid Poppy is one of those children."

Instantly, Erica couldn't breathe, a steel band compressing her lungs. "Oh God. I-I'm coming down there. I'm leaving now."

She was vaguely aware that she was panicking. She was on her feet, knowing she needed to find her car keys and her bag, but her brain didn't seem to be communicating properly with her body, and instead she paced back and forth, unsure of what she was doing.

"Mrs Swift?" the voice on the phone said.

It had been so long since anyone had called her that, she almost didn't recognise her own name. "I'm sorry, what?"

"I was just saying that the children are unharmed, and we're in contact with them."

Erica forced herself to think, to remember to ask the right questions. "How long have they been down there?"

"It's been a couple of hours now."

Her jaw dropped. "A couple of hours! And you're only calling me now?"

The woman's voice was hesitant. "We were hoping for this to be resolved without involving the parents right away."

"Jesus Christ. This isn't a couple of kids having an argument. You should have contacted us immediately. I could be there by now!"

"We had no way of knowing how serious the situation would become. I truly am sorry."

Erica was furious. "Sorry is no fucking good!"

She couldn't help but picture her daughter trapped in a dark tunnel somewhere. How frightened was she? Did they have light? Water and food? Air?

She stopped pacing and doubled over, forcing herself to take some breaths and calm herself. She dealt with emergency situations all the time. It was her job. It was very different when it involved the most important person in the world to her, though.

"Okay, how long until the man is freed?"

"We don't know that yet," Dawn said.

"And are the children safe until then?"

"Yes, they're safe for now."

Erica echoed her words. "For now?"

"There is a concern that the level of oxygen will start to decrease. The group leader is blocking the way, so reducing the air flow."

Panic rose again, and she fought it down.

Dawn continued, "The rescuers are doing everything they can. We'll pipe in air, if necessary."

Everything they can... How often had she used that phrase herself? Yes, they might be, but it didn't mean they were going to be successful, though, did it?

"I'm on my way."

Erica ended the call, her mind spinning.

Maybe she should have called Natasha. She was Poppy's aunt, after all, and practically helped raise her, but Erica found the first person she wanted to speak to was Shawn. He was the one she wanted to have by her side.

What if he didn't answer or he was busy? How would she cope without him? She needed him with her.

But he answered on the second ring, and everything she knew flooded from her mouth.

"Holy shit," he said. "I'll be right there."

She ended the call and phoned her sister. She didn't want Natasha to find out via the local news or social media. Natasha loved Poppy and would rightfully be seriously pissed off if she didn't hear about what was happening directly from Erica.

Erica filled Natasha in. Understandably, Natasha was distraught and wanted to be there, but she had her own children to look after.

"I have to go. I need to pack some things for Poppy before Shawn gets here."

"Okay," Natasha said. "Keep me updated. I'm going to be sick with worry."

"I will."

A part of her wished she could go and not have to wait for Shawn, but she knew she wouldn't be able to do this without him. Leaning on another person wasn't something she always found easy, but right now she needed him. She needed to lean on him with her whole weight, and he was strong enough to hold her up.

She raced around the house, shoving things she thought Poppy might need into a bag. It was pointless—Poppy had already taken everything she'd needed with her on the residential—but it gave her something to do. She also checked her phone every thirty seconds, desperate for an update, while also being terrified to get bad news.

A car pulled up outside.

Shawn didn't even bother to knock or ring the bell. He still had the key she'd given him.

"Erica?" His voice came from down the stairs.

"I'm here."

She grabbed the bag and hurried down to meet him. "Shawn?" His name cracked on her lips.

"Oh, shit, Erica."

He wrapped her in his arms in a fierce hug.

"I should never have let her go," she sobbed onto his chest. "Why did I let her go?"

"Stop, this isn't your fault. You had no way of knowing this would happen."

There was no point in arguing with him. She forced herself to pull away and wiped her face. "We have to go."

The site was a couple of hours' drive away.

"I'm driving," Shawn told her. "You're in no state."

She shook all over, her hands practically vibrating. How would she manage a two-hour drive? What if she didn't get there quickly enough and Poppy died without her being there? She didn't think she'd be able to cope. There would be no point in continuing.

Her heart would stop beating the moment's Poppy's did.

The drive down to the location was the longest of her life. She stared at her phone the whole time, chewing on the nails of her free hand, desperate for news. Local reporters had got hold of the story, and people were posting about it on social media as well. Some were likening the rescue mission to the one that had taken place in Thailand with the football team of boys, but Erica prayed it was nothing like that. She'd watched the documentary about that rescue and had seen that the boys were lucky to come out of the cave with their lives. The thought of Poppy going through something similar absolutely killed Erica.

After what felt like a lifetime, they finally arrived.

The area was a hive of activity. Ambulances were on standby. Police vehicles and uniformed officers had created a cordon to prevent nosey locals from getting too close and interfering with the rescue mission. To one side, news vans and reporters had gathered, eager to snap up even a morsel of information that might be thrown to them.

Erica threw herself out of the car before Shawn had even had the chance to switch off the engine and ran towards the nearest uniformed officer.

She was out of breath when she reached him, though she was sure it was more from panic than exertion. "My daughter is Poppy Swift," she said. "She's one of the trapped children."

The police officer offered her a smile of sympathy. "The rescue team are doing everything they can to get her out. The tent over there is for families of the children. We'll get you news as soon as we can."

It wasn't really a tent, more a canvas gazebo. She glanced over to see worried parents gathered beneath it. Several were crying, being comforted by partners or grandparents.

She became aware of Shawn behind her.

"I'm Detective Sergeant Turner, and this is Detective Inspector Swift," he said, holding up his ID for the uniformed officer to see. "We'd like to talk to whoever is in charge."

The officer shifted uncomfortably. "I understand, but I've been told to send family over to the tent."

"Just five minutes," Shawn pressed. "It's important."

The officer thinned his lips, and then gave a curt nod and stepped back.

"Thank you," Shawn said. "Who are we asking for?"

"Sergeant Combs. He's the one standing over there." The officer nodded in the sergeant's direction.

Erica felt his hand on her lower back, urging her forwards. She got her feet moving and ducked beneath the cordon.

She was grateful for Shawn's involvement. She'd always assumed she'd be on the ball in situations like this, but instead she found she was utterly numb and unable to string a thought together. Her brain buzzed with the terror of losing her daughter, and she could barely get her body to respond.

"Who are you?" the sergeant asked, a frown furrowing his face.

Erica found her voice. "I'm DI Swift with the Met Police. My daughter is one of the children trapped down there. This is my partner, DS Turner."

The sergeant's features softened, and he placed his hand on her shoulder. "I really am sorry you and your daughter are going through this. We're doing everything we can."

Erica wanted to scream at him to tell people to stop saying that. She told herself she'd never say that line to another person in distress ever again.

"How far are the rescue team from the children?" Shawn asked.

"They're with them now, but we need to free the tour guide before we can lead the children safely out."

"Shouldn't there be two ways in and out of these tunnels? That can't be the only way for them to get out," Erica said.

"You're right, there is. They got into the caving system via another entrance point, but the problem we have is that they're far closer to the exit point here than they are the entrance."

"I can't see the problem. Why can't they go back if nothing's blocking them that way?"

"It's over a mile of very narrow tunnels. A mile might not seem like a lot, but when you're down there in the dark, it feels like it. The issue we have is that there isn't enough space for anyone to turn around—not the children or the rescuers—so if they try to get out that way, they'll be crawling backwards. These tunnels are hard enough to navigate, without adding that into the mix. Plus we've got five panicky and upset children. The rescuers are worried that it'll cause more harm than good if they attempt it."

"But what about the oxygen. Won't they run out down there?"

"We're still working on freeing the guide, but the children are safe for the moment. We'll take action long before they run out of air, okay?"

Erica wasn't okay. She wasn't okay at all, but she just nodded. She hated feeling so helpless.

She wished she hadn't agreed to there being no contact between her and Poppy while on the residential. What if at the coach the other morning had been the last time she'd ever speak to her daughter? She hoped Poppy had at least read the notes Erica had put in her bag, the ones telling her how much she was loved, and how proud Erica was of her. If Poppy didn't make it out of this, and Erica found the notes unopened, she thought she'd implode with grief.

They left Sergeant Combs and joined the other families.

A trestle table had been erected, and someone had brought in a hot water urn to make teas and coffees with.

Erica recognised some of the parents and exchanged words of sympathy with them. She'd never been very involved with the school—something she'd often felt guilty about—and didn't know the other children's parents in a way they seemed to know each other. She was aware that plenty of people had assumed Natasha was Poppy's mum, since she was often the one who did the school pickups and drop-offs and arranged the playdates. It made Erica feel like less of a parent, but what could she do? Her job was important, too, and she suspected she minded more than Poppy ever had.

Time seemed to drag past without any news.

"Can I get you something to eat?" Shawn offered. "You need to keep your strength up."

She shook her head. "I can't eat. My stomach is in knots."

She received a message from Natasha and updated her, though there wasn't much she was able to tell.

What if it got dark and the children were still down there? She guessed it wouldn't make much difference to those inside the tunnels, since it was dark down there anyway, but what would they do? The caving system was miles from the actual property where the residential had been taking place. There wasn't much around here at all apart from the caves and fields and a river running through them. She got the feeling the police would try to encourage them to find hotels nearby, but there was no way Erica would leave this spot. She'd camp out here all night if she had to.

A radio crackled.

"That's excellent news," the sergeant said.

Erica's hear pounded, and she stood straight, trying to get an idea about what was being said.

"The rescue team have been able to free the guide."

His family had been kept a distance away from the parents. Erica hadn't even noticed them until this point. All she'd been focused on was the children, not giving the trapped man or his family any thought. They must have been worried sick, too, but they'd been kept away from the parents, most likely in case one of them decided this was all the guide's fault and took their fear and frustration out on his family. People didn't always think straight in these situations.

Everyone waited with bated breath.

Movement came at the opening to the tunnels, and then, as though he was being born again by the rock face, one of the rescue team slithered out and then reached back to pull out a kind of flexible stretcher that the guide was strapped onto.

Some people cheered, while others shouted, "What about the children? When are they coming out?"

The man's arm was in a sling. He had bloodied scrapes across his face, though his helmet was still in place. It had probably saved him if the rockfall had come from overhead.

He was clearly distraught.

"I'm so sorry I've left them behind." He directed his words towards the parents, while police kept them back.

"You were supposed to be watching our kids!" one of the fathers shouted.

Erica turned to the father. "And he was, but he had no control over part of the tunnel roof collapsing, did he?"

She didn't wait for a reply but approached Sergeant Combs instead.

"How is he?" she asked.

"He's suffered a broken arm and a dislocated shoulder from where the rockfall trapped him, but he's going to be fine."

"Are the children able to get past the rockfall?"

"The rescuers are still working on it. We need to make sure the ceiling isn't going to come down when they pass through. It's clearly unstable. We don't want to risk any of the children ending up injured or trapped."

They're already trapped, she wanted to say but didn't.

"Does anyone know what caused it?" she asked instead.

"Possibly a tiny earthquake that wouldn't have been felt by us but would have been enough to shift the rock structure and cause the fall. There's no way anyone could have predicted this happening."

Erica understood that, but when anything like this happened, people were always looking for someone to blame.

The wait continued, and it was the longest of her life. They were all desperate for even the tiniest morsel of news.

After more than an hour, Sergeant Combs approached them. His expression seemed lighter, the hint of a smile touching the corners of his lips. "I just got word that they're starting to move the children."

A ripple of relief went through the small crowd.

"Oh, thank God," Erica said.

She turned to Shawn, who pulled her into a hug.

"She's going to be okay," he said against the top of her head.

She wanted to believe that, but until she had Poppy back in her arms again, she couldn't bring herself to relax fully.

One by one, the children emerged from the tunnels, each one helped by a member of the rescue team. Erica watched out, desperate to see her daughter, and her heart fell with disappointment every time one of the other families got to rush forward and hold their child.

Finally, she spotted her—the last child to appear.

"Oh my God, Poppy."

She raced forwards and grabbed her.

"Mummy!"

She squeezed her daughter tight and kissed the top of her head only to find the helmet still in the way. "I'm so happy you're okay." Erica created space between them so she could look into her daughter's face. "You are okay, aren't you?"

"Yes, I'm okay."

But tears shone in the girl's eyes, and her chin wobbled, like it did when she was trying not to cry.

"It's okay, Poppy. You don't need to be brave in front of me."

"You're always brave." Poppy sniffed.

Erica gave a small laugh. "No, I'm really not. When I heard about you being trapped in those tunnels, I was so frightened, I couldn't even string a thought together. Shawn had to come and rescue me."

Poppy smiled in his direction. "Thanks for rescuing Mum, Shawn."

"Anytime."

A cleared throat nearby drew their attention.

Sergeant Combs jerked his head at the waiting ambulance. "I hate to interrupt the reunion, but all the children will need to be checked over by paramedics."

Poppy's eyes went wide. "I don't want to go to hospital."

"Are you hurt anywhere?" Erica asked her.

"No, I'm fine. Honest."

"You won't need to stay overnight, Poppy," the sergeant said. "It'll only be a checkup, and then you'll be able to go home."

"We won't get to finish the residential?" The corners of her mouth dipped in disappointment.

Erica almost laughed. "Would you really want to?"

"Yeah. We were having fun until the caving thing."

"I think the residential is probably going to be postponed now, love. It was your last day tomorrow anyway, remember?"

There would be an investigation into what had happened. Erica doubted the place would be taking in any more school groups anytime soon.

"Yeah, I suppose." Poppy shrugged her narrow shoulders.

"And honestly, I'd really like to have you home."

"Haven't you got to work?"

Guilt lifted its head and lashed its tail. "No, we just finished with a case. I think it's time I was owed a few days off. What do you think?"

"That sounds good."

The paramedics came over to check Poppy. They made a big fuss of her, and Poppy was grinning within seconds.

Erica suddenly realised she hadn't told Natasha that Poppy was safe. Natasha would be almost as worried as Erica had been, and she felt bad that she hadn't immediately thought of her sister. She took her phone from her pocket and made the call, filling her in on the few details she had. The whole family was relieved.

The sergeant touched Erica's elbow and lowered his voice. "We will need to speak to Poppy about what happened and get her statement. Of course, you can be in the room with her when that happens. There will be an investigation to make sure all the correct procedures were followed."

"I'm just grateful that no one was seriously hurt."

"Yes, things could have ended differently, that's for sure. Maybe we can have a chat with Poppy at the hospital, if that's all right with you."

She offered him a tight-lipped smile. "I'm sure that'll be fine, as long as it won't take too long. We're all keen to get home as soon as possible."

"Of course. It's been a long day for everyone. I bet we could all do with a rest."

He really had no idea.

Erica glanced over to where Poppy was sitting in the back of the ambulance. She didn't seem too badly affected by what she'd been through. She was still talking nineteen to the dozen, telling the paramedics everything that had happened, before and after the tunnel ceiling had caved in. The thought of it still sickened Erica. The sergeant had been right when he'd said things could have ended differently. What if Poppy had been the one under the rockfall? It could have crushed her.

She shook the thought from her head. It wasn't going to help anyone to torture herself with images of something that hadn't happened.

"I'll ride in the ambulance with her," Erica said to Shawn. "If you could drive the car over there. Hopefully, they'll give us the all-clear, and Poppy can give her statement, and then we can go home."

"Of course." His arm slid around her shoulders, and he pulled her in for a hug. "She's safe now. You can breathe."

She nodded against him. "I know, thanks. I'll see you there."

• • • •

A FEW HOURS LATER, they were on their way back to London.

Poppy dozed in the back seat, clearly exhausted by what she'd been through. Erica was shattered, too. Shawn drove, and she allowed herself to rest the side of her head on his shoulder and let her eyelids close. It felt right, the three of them being together like this.

When they arrived home, Shawn carried Poppy from the car. Poppy woke up, and Erica got her a snack before giving her a bath and putting her to bed. Shawn stayed downstairs, giving the two of them some space.

"Is Shawn going to stay here tonight?" Poppy asked. "It's a bit late for him to be going home, isn't it?"

"How would you feel about that? I mean, if Shawn was maybe having the occasional sleepover..."

Poppy's eyebrows shot up her forehead. "Sleepovers? Is Shawn your boyfriend now, Mum?"

Erica's cheeks flared with heat. "I mean, using the word boyfriend feels a little strange when you're our age, but I guess you could say that. We're seeing how things go."

Poppy grinned. "It's okay, Mum. I'm happy if Shawn is your boyfriend. You deserve to have a boyfriend. It's not like you're old and crusty yet."

"Thanks, Pops." She paused and then added, "And if you've got any questions or worries, I want you to feel you can share them with me, okay? Because if you've got questions and worries, I can guarantee that I'll be having them, too, and it's always much better to give them a voice than keep them buried inside you."

Poppy grew solemn for once. "I know, Mum, but I am really happy about this, I promise. It's like we'll finally be a real family again."

Erica tried not to feel the stab of pain, grief, and guilt her words conjured. She failed. "We've always been a real family, Poppy. Families come in all shapes and sizes."

"Yeah, I know, but I think I'll still like it better."

"There's one more thing," Erica said. "Because I'm technically Shawn's boss, we can't let everyone know, okay? Family are fine, but no work people. If you see me with another police officer, you mustn't mention anything."

Poppy screwed up her face. "Eww, as if I'm going to talk about your boyfriend to someone you work with."

Erica laughed. "Okay, okay. Point taken." She kissed Poppy's forehead and tucked in the covers. "Get some sleep. I love you."

Poppy's eyes were already closed, so Erica slipped out of the room and went downstairs.

"I need a drink," Erica said to Shawn. "I don't care that it's the middle of the night. You want one, too?"

"If I have a drink, I won't be able to drive anywhere tonight."

"That's fine, Shawn. You don't have to go anywhere if you don't want to."

"I don't want to," he replied.

"Good." She paused and then said, "I want to thank you for today, Shawn. I honestly don't know how I would have coped without you."

"You'd have coped fine. You're the strongest person I know."

She shook her head. "No, I'm not always strong. Sometimes it feels like I'm going to crumble into a million pieces if I allow myself to show even the slightest crack. I meant what I said. You've been my rock today." She gave a small laugh. "You're always my rock. I don't know what I'd do without you."

He stepped in closer. "And I'll always be here, Erica. No matter what. If you want me, I'm here."

She finally allowed herself to admit something she'd felt for a long time. "I do want you, Shawn. I do."

Chapter Thirty-Three

Richard Morrisey lifted his coffee cup to his lips and noted how his hand trembled, sending tiny ripples across the brown liquid.

He let out a sigh and set the mug back down again. Nothing had been normal since he'd got back home. His whole belief that he was safe and secure in society had been shaken to its core.

Though he loved being back around his family, it wasn't easy. Every night, his sleep was plagued with nightmares. Sometimes, he was the one still chained in that room, but other times he'd be on the other side of the door, and it would be his wife or one of the children who were in that chair, the water rising around their feet. He'd hammer on the door and try to get people to help, but it was as though no one was listening, and he'd wake up, a scream lodged in his throat or peeling from between his lips.

He was going to start counselling soon, but he couldn't imagine telling a therapist the details of what he'd actually been through, how he'd been forced to piss and shit himself while sitting in that goddamned chair, how he'd cried like a child, believing he was going to die. He'd never known pain like it, having to sit in that same position for almost three days, every muscle in his body howling with agony. He'd suffered cramps like he'd never experienced before, like knives being plunged into his calves and neck and back, and his eyes had filled with tears, and he'd gritted his teeth and clamped down on the cry rising inside him.

Now he jumped at the slightest noise, and the sound of the taps running or even dripping sent him into a panic. His heartbeat banging, his palms prickling with sweat. He saw danger in life in a way he never had before.

It was even worse that so many people had seen him at his most vulnerable moment. Now he felt exposed, as though everyone in the street had watched him on the toilet or having sex with his wife. People seemed to know who he was, and he didn't know if he was being paranoid, but he felt as though everyone was whispering about him behind their hands. The press had been hounding them as well, trying to get an exclusive inside scope on what he'd been through. He didn't plan on reliving that horror with anyone. He couldn't even bring himself to speak the full truth of it to his wife.

When he'd been in his darkest moments, he'd even wondered why he'd been chosen instead of his wife. Everyone said the kidnappings had been politically motivated, but he wasn't the politician, his wife was. It should have been her who suffered through all of that. But then as soon as the thought crossed his mind, he forced it away again. He loved Nancy, and he would never have wanted someone else he loved to have gone through that. In some ways, maybe it had been even worse for his wife and children than it had been for him.

Nancy came in, reading her phone, a frown furrowing her forehead.

"Everything all right?" he asked.

The words felt hollow to him. He even resented asking the question. Why would everything be all right? It should be her asking that about him.

Nancy didn't glance up. "It looks as though the site we'd earmarked for the windfarm in the North Sea is being dropped."

"Why?"

"I'm not sure. Possibly connections with the climate change group who were responsible for what happened with you. A lot of the investors are pulling out. They don't want their names, or the names of their companies, associated with them."

Richard snorted. "I can't say I blame them."

"It's just surprised me. I wasn't expecting things to go this way."

"It's what you want, though, isn't it?" Richard said. "You were always saying about how we're all having to bend to the will of all these greenies to try and make ourselves acceptable in their eyes."

She still seemed concerned. "Yes, I suppose so."

"You sound unsure."

"It's good for the party. Offshore Solutions wouldn't be able to make such a big donation this year if they hadn't got this contract. I guess I don't like the idea that we're benefitting in some way from what you and the others went through. That poor woman lost her life."

"Yes, but that's not our fault. It's the fault of The Climate Uprising."

"They still haven't arrested anyone for it, though, have they?" she said.

"They arrested two of them. It's in the papers."

"For assault on someone else, though. I know the papers have made it sound like it was for what happened, but it says it's connected to the case, not that they're to blame for it."

She had a point. Why hadn't the police been able to arrest the person or people responsible for what had happened to him? The thought that they were still out there somewhere kept him awake at night.

What if they decided to finish the job?

Chapter Thirty-Four

Within days of his rescue, Hector Townsend was appearing on news bulletins and television chat shows. He already seemed remarkably better. Though he was still extremely thin, the colour had returned to his face, and his eyes seemed brighter.

He was certainly no shrinking violet. He must have given interviews to anyone who asked, and, despite the police requesting that he kept the details to himself, it was clear he was a talker. The public lapped it up, hanging on his every word. There were even calls for there to be more stringent laws to be brought in to prevent the creation of groups like The Climate Uprising and make it illegal for anyone to join. Of course, this only got activists more up in arms, and over the next week there were a number of protests in London, and other cities as well, where both sides clashed and things turned violent. It did nothing to help their cause, however, and only proved Hector's point that these groups were essentially no better than terrorists.

The whole thing made Erica uncomfortable. Something about it made her feel as though the climate groups had been pitched against the police, but then that was nothing new. Trouble was that now the climate groups were looking like violent criminals and yobs, and those who were against them used the murder of poor Catherine Taura as proof.

"Do you ever get the feeling you're being manipulated?" she said to Shawn one morning over a very early breakfast.

The news was on in the background, reporting on the latest bout of protests and fighting that had hit the city. This latest one had occurred because of a U-turn the government had just taken on the windfarm that had been due to be built in the North Sea over the next few years rather than a new oil field being drilled.

He raised an eyebrow. "That would depend on who by."

She waved a hand at the television. "This all seems a bit convenient, doesn't it?"

"In what way?"

"A big oil company loses a contract to a windfarm company, and then people connected to the oil company in some way are kidnapped and put through hell, and even killed, and the decision is reversed. The argument is that the climate change group targeted those people because of their connection to the oil company, but in the end it's had the reverse effect of what they'd intended on achieving."

"It's often that way, though, isn't it? I mean, not to this kind of extreme, but the things they do often turn the public against them. They don't always do themselves any favours."

"No, but they get people talking, and that's what they want."

He threw up a hand. "Well, there you go then. Nothing has ever got people talking on such a level as this, so even though a decision went against them, they still got what they wanted."

"Don't you think it's strange that we haven't been able to pin this on anyone, though? Yes, we know the group behind it because we've been told, but as for actual hard proof? The Climate Uprising are denying having anything to do with it, which is understandable since a woman was murdered, but we haven't had anyone come forward to claim responsibility. No one we've looked into matches the profile of who we're after. None of it makes sense. Plus we've got two survivors, and neither of them have been any help whatsoever in trying to help us narrow down who took them. How can they not have seen anything? It's frustrating."

Richard's statement was simply that he recalled coming back home after dropping the children off at school but that he remembered nothing after that until he woke up in the room, chained to the chair.

Hector was a little different, in that he said he was doing a site visit when someone knocked him unconscious from behind. Again, he didn't see anyone and only remembered waking up in that room to find himself locked in there.

Because the site wasn't being used for anything while they fought with the council about planning, the number of security cameras around the site had been minimal, and even then only stayed online for twenty-four hours before they were wiped again. Hector had given the police access to all the footage they had, but there was nothing useful. Erica questioned the positioning of some of the cameras, wondering why they were where they were, but Hector had commented that if he'd known something like this was remotely likely to happen, he'd have made different choices.

Whoever had gone to the effort of creating the sauna and sealing up the rooms must have noted where the cameras were and done whatever was needed to avoid them.

She'd thought the construction of the sauna would have been difficult, but it turned out that it was surprisingly simple. It was essentially an insulated shed with a heat source, and it was easy enough to buy a kit online. Plenty of them claimed that if someone had a halfway decent knowledge of construction, a sauna kit could be built in less than twenty-four hours.

It meant that there was no point in trying to follow up with leads as far as hoping a local company might have built it.

• • • •

ERICA HADN'T FORGOTTEN the young woman who'd helped them with the case. She picked up the phone and called Jasmin.

The girl answered after a few rings. "Hello?"

"Hi, Jasmin, it's Erica. Erica Swift. I just wanted to thank you again for helping with the case. You really were key to cracking it. I don't know what we would have done without you. I suspect we'd have lost Richard Morrisey and Hector Townsend, too."

"I wish I'd been faster. Maybe I'd have been able to save Catherine, too."

"None of this is your fault. Without you, we'd have had a very different ending."

"I'm glad I was of help. I can't help going back over everything, wondering if I could have done things differently." She paused and then added, "To be honest, I'm surprised we managed to crack it at all. I didn't think we were going to. I got lucky with the malware getting through. It was almost as though someone deliberately removed the encryption for a few seconds to let me in."

Erica let her words hang and then said, "What do you mean?"

"I'm not sure. It was all completely locked down, and then suddenly it wasn't."

"*Could* it have been done deliberately?" Erica wondered.

"Possibly, but why would they do that?"

"Someone got cold feet?"

"Maybe."

Erica cleared her throat. "Well, if you ever decide you want to work for the police, I'll be sure to put in a good word for you. We could do with more people with your skills."

"Thanks, boss," Jas said.

Erica could hear the grin in her voice.

They ended the call, but Jasmin's words stayed with her. Had someone really allowed them in so they could find the location of the victims before it was too late? She thought again about Hector Townsend, about how this whole thing had made him both a celebrity and a lot of money. Richard Morrisey had reacted in the opposite way—not wanting to speak to anyone. Yes, Hector had suffered terribly, but hadn't things gone his way in the end?

She decided to dig a little deeper into Hector. She wasn't sure what this feeling was leading her towards, but she knew to trust her gut when it was trying to tell her something.

Erica found some recent footage of him on YouTube.

"We can't let groups like this try to control our lives," Hector said into a fluffy black microphone that was being held out to him. "We've seen how dangerous they can be. Enough is enough."

A news reporter asked a question. "Do you think the recent U-turn on the windfarm was the right thing to do then?"

"I think we were left with no choice. We can't be seen giving these people what they want."

The reporter seemed to agree, as she turned back to the camera to speak directly into it. "Support for the new drilling field in the North Sea is at an all-time high. Where previously it looked as though the application was going to be turned down in favour of a windfarm, mainly due to concerns about fossil fuel use, it now seems as though plans will be going ahead. The company was due to lose billions of pounds of investment if it didn't."

"Everything okay?" Shawn asked her. "You've got one hell of a serious expression."

She jumped straight in. "Do you see how Hector Townsend is all over the news and social media?"

"Yeah, he's doing much better, isn't he. Almost unrecognisable to the man we rescued."

"I can't help wondering if it's all a little too convenient."

"What do you mean?"

"Well, everyone's treating him like a bit of a hero, aren't they? Now he has this big platform that he's using to push a company that he's got a lot of money invested in, and it's worked."

"I mean, it's understandable, isn't it? It's not his fault he got elevated to some celebrity status."

"Yes, but he's using that platform to speak out against The Climate Uprising, and any other climate change groups who might stand up for them, when we don't actually know who was behind what happened to him yet. We haven't made any arrests, despite our best efforts, but he's telling the world that they were definitely the ones responsible."

"You can't blame him. He believes what he's saying is true."

She tilted her head. "Does he, though? Don't you think it's strange how no one has come forward and claimed responsibility for what happened? Why go to all that trouble but then not use the platform it creates? The only person who has is Hector."

"Maybe because they didn't get what they wanted? If we hadn't found the victims, perhaps they would have spoken out."

Erica couldn't let it go. "Something else is bothering me. Jasmin said it was as though they removed all their encryption right at the last moment and gave her access."

"So, it was probably a glitch, and we were lucky enough to have someone who knew what they were doing to be monitoring it at the right moment. If she hadn't been, and they fixed the glitch right away, then we might never have even known it had happened."

"Or it was done on purpose? They knew we had someone trying to trace the origin and someone wanted us to find out."

Shawn's eyebrows drew together. "Why would they do that?"

"Because they never planned on killing the victims?"

"I don't understand."

She rubbed her hand over her mouth. "I'm not sure I do either. I just don't like the way this has gone. It's not right."

Shawn seemed to think for a moment. "Did Nancy Morrisey have any direct connection with Hector?"

"Not that I'm aware of. I mean, he had shares in a company that donated millions to her party, but that's all." She gave a cold laugh. "You'd think it would be a conflict of interest to take money from an oil company."

"It's not as though she took the money directly."

Erica raised an eyebrow. "That we know of." She tapped her fingers against her thigh. "It would certainly give her a reason to want people to turn against green energy, if she wanted the money from the oil company to keep rolling in. They could do that by turning the people who support the fight against climate change into the real enemy. By discrediting them. Making them into the monsters."

He stared at her. "You understand what you're saying here? That Nancy did that to her own husband?"

Erica remembered how shocked the woman had been, how distressed. She didn't seem to have known about it. "Okay, maybe not Nancy then, but someone has benefitted from this. In fact, a lot of people have, including Hector Townsend. Not only are his share prices rocketing, but he's become a minor celebrity."

"You can't think he did this to himself? That he starved himself, almost to death, in order to get this contract."

"It was worth billions. And he didn't do this on his own. If it wasn't Nancy, maybe it was someone close to her."

Shawn shook his head. "There's no way Richard Morrisey was in on it either. That man was genuinely terrified that he was going to die. Did you see him when we eventually freed him? He was hysterical. He couldn't even walk. And he's got two children. I don't think anyone would do that willingly, even when there's billions of pounds involved."

"I'd suggest Catherine, since she worked for Offshore Solutions, but I highly doubt she'd have put herself in a situation that killed her." She ran her tongue across her teeth and let out a breath. "Shit. It has to be Hector, and maybe someone in government. It's the only thing that makes sense. I'm going to have to run this by Gibbs. I can't go accusing a political party of conspiring like that. It's going to send shock waves through the country if it's true."

"We have to do something," Shawn agreed. "If you're correct about this, it's not right that an innocent organisation is being blamed."

"Thank God we never had enough proof to charge any of them."

Shawn pointed at her. "That's another thing. Why was there no proof? If they'd been guilty of what happened, we'd have pinned it on them. All we had was the accusations from a man who wasn't able to name names but was able to accuse the organisation, nonetheless."

"See," Erica said. "It's all too convenient." She thought for a moment and remembered something else that had niggled at her. "Hector said he'd been left with supplies but no one had been back to see him, but that can't be true because his door was unlocked when we found him. They wouldn't have left it unlocked when he'd first been taken because he'd been strong enough to walk right out of there, so he's lying about something."

"Or someone unlocked it when he was asleep?" Shawn suggested.

"But why would they do that?"

The general public had also been divided on the matter. Protests against both sides had sprung up on the streets, and on occasions, things had got heated. It meant the police were forced to step in, and the waters were already muddied as to who should or shouldn't be arrested due to recent changes in the 'right to protest' legislation. Something like climate change—something that would affect them all—had become even more of a triggering topic.

"Let's dig deeper into Hector Townsend," she said. "See what we can find."

Erica got onto it as well. While Hector might have been considered a bit of a recluse prior to the abduction, he still had pages of photographs come up when she searched his name.

She stopped on one of the photographs. She recognised the man standing a couple of feet behind Hector.

Wasn't that Daniel Southern?

Had Daniel worked for Hector at some point?

Suddenly, everything fell into place. The body shape was exactly right from the footage in the stairwell when Catherine had been taken. No wonder she hadn't stood any chance in fighting against a man with his kind of size and strength, plus he had the training to know how to disable someone.

Could Hector and Daniel have been in this together? Daniel would have known Richard's movements, maybe even had access to the security cameras at the house, and even been able to get hold of a key. He'd have had to move fast so Richard didn't see him, but then they'd suspected that of happening.

But there had been a second man in the CCTV footage from the parking garage when Catherine had been taken. They knew that couldn't have been Hector. He was in regular shape—not half-starved.

Erica filled her team in on what she'd found.

"Let's find out if Daniel Southern has received any large payments recently," she said. "If he was involved, I suspect he wasn't only doing it for the good of the party, or to help Nancy Morrisey out."

"I'll file a request for bank information," Shawn said.

They needed to speak to the two men and find out if Erica's suspicions were founded.

Chapter Thirty-Five

In Interview Room One, Hector Townsend sat behind a table. Shawn was running the interview.

In the room next door, with Erica, was Daniel Southern.

The man glared at Erica. Beside him sat a solicitor who probably charged more per hour than some people earned in a week.

As well as the history that Daniel shared with Hector, Erica's team had found an offshore account in Daniel's name with one million pounds recently deposited in it. Five hundred grand was put in shortly before Hector went missing, and the other five hundred appeared not long after Hector had been found.

They were able to trace the money back to one of the company accounts Hector Townsend ran.

Erica had already run through the groundwork of the interview and had read him his rights.

Daniel sat back, his arms folded across his chest defensively. "This is bullshit. You know that, right? Whatever Hector Townsend has been saying about me is all lies."

"Why would you assume Mr Townsend has said something?"

"I figured you'd dug a little deeper and seen that I used to work for him. What other reason would you have to arrest me?"

"Oh, trust me," Erica said. "We have our reasons. I'll get to that shortly."

"It's all bullshit," he repeated.

"We'll see about that. It's come to light that no one abducted Mr Townsend, that, in fact, he put himself in that room, starved himself, and made it look as though the group, The Climate Uprising, was responsible. He also arranged to have Catherine Taura and Richard Morrisey abducted, but then I suspect you already know that."

"I don't know anything."

"That ring you're wearing," she nodded to the gold signet on his left hand, "have you had it long?"

"Yeah. It was a birthday present from my dad when I turned twenty-one."

Erica turned her laptop so he could see the screen. On it was a screenshot of the CCTV footage from Catherine Taura's place of work. It had been focused in on the hand of the man driving the white van—the same one that was suspected of abducting her. "Wouldn't you say that's the same ring?"

He shrugged. "I bet there are thousands of those rings made. It doesn't prove anything."

She pulled up a shot from the stairwell, where Catherine had been grabbed. A part of her was kicking herself for not recognising his build sooner, but he looked so different in casual clothes compared to his usual suit.

"Are you telling me that's not you in the picture?" she asked.

"It's not me, and if that's all you've got, you'd better let me go right now."

She gave him a polite smile, aware it didn't reach her eyes. "It's not all we've got, Daniel. It's merely part of a much bigger picture."

"I don't know what you're talking about."

She switched tactics. "Hector had a lot to gain by the windfarm contract being cancelled, but what did you stand to gain from it, Daniel? Was it only about the money?"

"What money?" He was still bluffing, but now he'd paled.

"Did Hector Townsend pay you a million pounds to help him kidnap Richard Morrisey and Catherine Taura, which resulted in Catherine's murder?"

"What? No!"

"We know about the million-pound deposit from Mr Townsend into an offshore account in your name. We know that you know about it, too. We can see that you've logged in to the account, and we can trace it back to the exact time and computer you used to log in. There's no point in denying it at this point. That information, together with the CCTV footage from the car park at Offshore Solutions, is impossible to argue."

Daniel glanced at his solicitor who clearly agreed with Erica.

Daniel's broad shoulders sank. "No one was supposed to get hurt, and yes, it was all about the money. Isn't everything? I didn't want the political party I've supported my whole life to go without millions of pounds just because of those bloody climate change people—it could cost them the election—and if I happened to make some on the side, even better."

"Whose idea was it to broadcast everything?" she asked.

"Hector's. We used an AI voice to speak into the rooms and over the footage. It wasn't difficult to do. Anyone can download a realistic AI voice these days, and we knew it wouldn't be traced back to us."

"There's one part of the puzzle I don't understand," Erica said. "You don't have the skills—as far as I'm aware—to create the kind of setup we had to deal with when trying to track where the feed was coming from."

"No, you're right. I know very little about all of that."

"So you had some help?"

His lips pinched, lines deepening around them. "I'm not a grass."

"You understand that you are being charged with two counts of abduction and imprisoning a person against their will, and one count of murder. Maybe if you help us, we can consider a deal."

He scoffed. "I'm not stupid, Detective. I'll be going away for a long time, no matter what."

"Perhaps, but this will make the judge look more favourably towards you. I think you need every bit of help you can get right now. We're going to find out eventually anyway."

He gave a sly smile. "Let's just say you need to look a bit closer to home."

"What do you mean by that?"

"It was important to get the timings right, to make sure you found Hector and the others shortly before the timer ended. We needed to know that the police were on the correct track and that nothing was going to interfere with our plan. Like I said, it was never our intention for anyone to get hurt."

A penny dropped. "Someone who was close to us. Someone who knew what we were doing. Who could control things from the inside?"

Someone had leaked Jasmin's name. She hadn't wanted to believe it had been from the inside, but she'd been wrong. Maybe that same person had even given Gordie Carol and

Tommy Biel a shove in the right direction to help cement their case? There was only one person who came to mind.

"Not Karl Hartley?"

She'd worked with Karl for years. She didn't think him capable of it. But then how well did she really know him? She remembered how angry he'd been about them bringing Jasmin in. She'd assumed it was because he'd been insulted, thinking that she thought he wasn't capable of doing his job, but maybe it was because he was worried she'd interfere with his plans.

Daniel shrugged. "You probably need to ask him that."

"Interview ended at," she said for the benefit of the recording and gave the time.

Erica stepped out into the corridor and signalled to Shawn in the room next door that she needed to talk to him.

"Daniel Southern is pointing the finger at Karl Hartley as their third accomplice."

Shawn's jaw dropped. "Our Karl Hartley?"

"Yes. It makes sense, if you think about it. They needed someone on the inside to make sure their timings were right."

"Damn."

"Let's be discreet about this. Everyone is going to find out eventually, but I don't want the whole office noticing that we're arresting him."

They went down to Karl's department. It was a smaller office, so at least they didn't need to worry about so many people noticing.

"Erica, what can I do for you?" He turned his head slightly and caught sight of Shawn standing there as well. Confusion and worry crossed his face. "Everything all right?"

"No, Karl, it's not. I think you know why we're here."

The colour drained from his face.

"Daniel Southern has pointed the finger at you, and I'm fairly sure Hector Townsend will corroborate."

"Shit," Karl cursed.

Erica took out her cuffs, and Shawn removed his jacket.

"Why did you do it, Karl?" she asked.

He hung his head. "Money problems. They promised me no one was going to get hurt, that they'd all be released within three days and no harm would come of it. It was such a lot of money, Erica. It blinded me. I couldn't say no. Besides, I always hated those stupid climate change protesters, holding everyone up on the roads and gluing themselves to things."

"Jesus, Karl." She was so disappointed in him. "Can you stand up? Put your hands in front of your body so I can cuff you. Shawn will put his jacket over the top so no one will see when we take you out of here."

Meekly, Karl did as she'd instructed.

"Karl Hartley," she said, "you're under arrest for kidnapping and false imprisonment of Richard Morrisey and Catherine Taura, and for the murder for Catherine Taura. You do not have to say anything. But, it may harm your defence if you do not mention when questioned something which you later rely on in court. Anything you do say may be given in evidence."

She couldn't take any pleasure in the arrest. Being betrayed by one of their own wasn't easy. But she was glad they knew the truth now. It would have been worse if he'd got away with it.

The people responsible were behind bars, and The Climate Uprising would have their names cleared.

The truth always came out in the end.

Acknowledgements

. . . .

THE JASMIN WEBB IN this book is, of course, a completely fictitious character. However, the person whose name I borrowed is definitely very real. Though I know she's been hankering after me making her a detective, with a name like Webb, I had to make her a hacker.

So thank you for letting me borrow your name, Jas! I hope you liked your character!

Thank you, as always, to my editor Emmy Ellis, and to my proofreaders, Jessica Fraser from Finishing by Fraser, Tammy Payne from Book Nook Nuts, and to Jacqueline Beard for always being that much needed final set of eyes. I promise I will get the next books in the post very soon.

Final thanks to you the reader, for sticking with Erica and Shawn. I hope the way this book concluded made you happy!

Until next time!

MK Farrar

About the Author

• • • •

M K FARRAR HAD PENNED more than twenty novels of psychological noir and crime fiction. A British author, she lives in the countryside with her three children and a menagerie of rescue pets.

When she's not writing—which isn't often—she balances out all the murder with baking and binge-watching shows on Netflix.

You can find out more about M K and grab a free book via her website, https://mkfarrar.com

She can also be emailed at mk@mkfarrar.com. She loves to hear from readers!

Also by the Author

DI Erica Swift Thriller

• • • •

Detective Ryan Chase Thriller

• • • •

1. https://www.amazon.co.uk/gp/product/B088KSCD4G

2. https://www.amazon.co.uk/gp/product/B088FYFCB3

3. https://www.amazon.co.uk/gp/product/B08B9QGXGR

4. https://www.amazon.co.uk/gp/product/B08G31DBNZ

5. https://www.amazon.co.uk/gp/product/B08L6XN1X1/

6. https://www.amazon.co.uk/gp/product/B0934N7FXZ

7. https://www.amazon.co.uk/dp/B08YH2L9LF

8. https://www.amazon.co.uk/gp/product/B098LCMVD2

9. https://www.amazon.co.uk/gp/product/B09JHZ4MP6

10. https://www.amazon.co.uk/gp/product/B09VCY9DTR

Crime After Crime
Watching Over Me[11]
Down to Sleep[12]
If I Should Die[13]

• • • •

Standalone Psychological Thrillers
Some They Lie[14]
On His Grave[15]
Down to Sleep[16]

11. https://books2read.com/u/mlLzOY

12. https://books2read.com/u/mKdBqv

13. https://books2read.com/u/ba6yXx

14. https://www.amazon.co.uk/gp/product/B07CPSSZ7D

15. https://www.amazon.co.uk/gp/product/B07Q6YBZQM

16. https://www.amazon.co.uk/gp/product/B07T63GK1K/

Printed in Great Britain
by Amazon

51884144R00155